The
Christmas
Note

Also by Donna VanLiere

The Christmas Journey

The Christmas Secret

Finding Grace

The Christmas Promise

The Angels of Morgan Hill

The Christmas Shoes

The Christmas Blessing

The Christmas Hope

Donna VanLiere

WITHDRAWN

The
Christmas
Note

St. Martin's Press
New York

This is a work of fiction. All of the characters, organizations, and events portrayed in this novel are either products of the author's imagination or are used fictitiously.

THE CHRISTMAS NOTE. Copyright © 2011 by Donna VanLiere. All rights reserved. Printed in the United States of America. For information, address St. Martin's Press, 175 Fifth Avenue, New York, N.Y. 10010.

www.stmartins.com

LIBRARY OF CONGRESS CATALOGING-IN-PUBLICATION DATA

VanLiere, Donna, 1966–
   The Christmas note / Donna VanLiere.—1st ed.
     p. cm.
   ISBN 978-0-312-65896-0
  1. Neighbors—Fiction. 2. Mothers—Death—Fiction. 3. Family secrets—Fiction. 4. Identity (Psychology)—Fiction. 5. Christmas stories.
I. Title.
  PS3622.A66C4787 2011
  813'.6—dc22

                                  2011025835

First Edition: November 2011

10 9 8 7 6 5 4 3 2 1

For my father, Archie,
who served in the navy

Acknowledgments

Special thanks to:

Troy, Gracie, Kate, and David for loving Christmas and keeping it crackling at our house.

Jen Gates and Esmond Harmsworth for your belief and passion.

Jen Enderlin, Matthew Baldacci, Michael Storrings, Rachel Ekstrom, and the St. Martin's sales staff for being outstanding in all that you do!

My longtime friend, Captain Bryan Ralls, United States Army, for guiding me through all things military. I appreciate your service to this country!

Mary Weekly for invaluable help and your gracious, sweet spirit.

Ann-Frances Barker, Carole Consiglio, Lynn Cook, Kim Cotton, Dawana Hunt, Dorothy Ley, Carri McPeek, Misty Riggs, Renee Sly, and Elizabeth Sweatt for your heart.

*The family you come from isn't as important as
the family you're going to have.*
—RING LARDNER

The
Christmas
Note

One

All things must change to something new, to something strange.

—HENRY WADSWORTH LONGFELLOW

GRETCHEN
November 30

I look out the window and wait, wondering what will happen today. Life is weird. Just when I think I'm making heads or tails of it, when I'm getting used to today, along comes a new morning. The kids are running through the condo screaming, listening to their own voices echo off the naked walls. As Ethan checks out every closet and cupboard space, his face is fixed in a wide, transforming smile, just like his father's. Emma is like me, more cautious as she looks, envisioning where her things will go. Her eyes flame

1

out fiery blue from her olive face as she swings her favorite stuffed animal, a bunny named Sugar, around her bedroom. When I was six, I had a stuffed dog named Henry. He's somewhere in the moving boxes. Ethan says that now that he's six he doesn't need a stuffed animal anymore, but I noticed he brought Friska the one-eared dog in the car with him. Seems all of us, no matter how old, have a hard time letting go sometimes.

The clouds look upset, puffing the sky up in a solid wall of gray. I hate moving when the trees have dropped their leaves. Everything's drab and bare and the feeling of emptiness chokes me. But that's today. Tomorrow will be different. "The truck is here!" I yell from the living-room window. My cell phone rings and I see that it's my mother. "It just pulled up," I say to her. "Bring your crew anytime."

I haven't lived near my mother since I left for college sixteen years ago, but Kyle and I always wanted to live closer to our parents; the trouble was always which one. Kyle's parents are still living in the small Oklahoma town where Kyle was raised, but I'd have to travel too far for work as a hygienist if we moved there. My parents are divorced. They decided when Jeff and I were teenagers that they couldn't live to-

gether anymore and it took me years to forgive them. I loved them always, but sometimes I couldn't stand to talk to either one of them because of what their decision did to our family. Dad lives in a town in Arizona near his children from his second failed marriage and enjoys his grandchildren there, but my mom doesn't live close to either Jeff or me. Not that she needed us; Miriam Lloyd-Davies stands just fine on her own, but I thought Emma and Ethan should be closer to her, three-blocks-away close, to be exact.

Ethan bolts past me and stands on the front stoop; it's not big enough to be called a porch. The builder planted some nondescript shrub in the spot by the door in a halfhearted attempt to make it feel homey. The garage door for the adjoining condo opens and I notice a car turning into the driveway. Ethan waves at the driver like he's been expecting her all day, and she pulls slowly up her drive, watching the moving men open the back of the truck, revealing all of our prized possessions. She stops her car and opens the door, staring at the movers without a hint of expression on her face. "Hi," I say, crossing my arms over my chest against the cold.

"We're moving in today," Ethan says, stepping closer to her. "What's your name?"

"Melissa." She's not heavy or thin, pretty or ugly. Her brown hair looks as if it was cut impatiently and her coat is too big for her. I can just see the tips of her fingers peeking from the sleeves.

"I'm Gretchen," I say, stepping next to Ethan. "My daughter Emma is in the house." She nods and I know she couldn't care less.

"Emma's eight," Ethan says. "Two years older than me. My dad was in the army. We have all sorts of medals that he won."

"Oh," Melissa says, dragging the *O* out and raising her shabby brown eyebrows and puckering her lips in that way people do when they don't approve of something: the soup, the new boyfriend, the performance of the car, the politician, or the way a new bra fits.

"All right," I say, turning Ethan toward the moving truck and away from Miss Personality. "Let's get busy." She doesn't offer to help or ask any questions of where we came from or how we ended up here, and from behind me I hear her garage door closing. I lead the men into the condo and point out where each box should go; in order to make today easier I had marked them with "kitchen," "bathroom,"

"bedroom 1," "bedroom 2," and "living room" as I packed up our former home.

Mom's car pulls in behind the truck, and she and her best friend Gloria step out. Mom is wearing black slacks and a soft green sweater. "Please tell me you're not unpacking boxes in angora, Mom," I say, walking toward the car. Ethan slams himself into her legs, and Gloria, although it's only been twelve weeks since I was here scoping out a place to live, greets me with one of her I-haven't-seen-you-in-twenty-years hugs. She's outfitted in what a normal person moves in: jeans and a lightweight cotton shirt.

"No matter what you're doing," Mom says, reaching for me, "there's never any reason to dress like a ruffian."

"That's what we are," Gloria says, looking at me. "Ruffians."

I'm still amazed that my mother and Gloria became best friends. Mom is all English with soft edges to her words and wardrobe, and Gloria is Georgia born and bred with fire in her soul and clothes from the thrift store, but they are good for each other. Gloria was widowed for more than a decade before marrying Marshall Wilson two years ago, but

somehow she and Mom still find time to prowl around and work together at Glory's Place, Gloria's center for single moms and their children.

Another car comes to a stop behind Mom, and four young guys step to the curb. I greet each one of them but know I won't remember any of their names ten minutes from now. My mind is inside each of those boxes and where the contents of each one needs to go. "Where'd you find all those guys?" I ask, watching them run up the ramp of the truck.

"Your mother still has a way with men," Mom says, kissing the top of Ethan's head.

Gloria laughs, walking to the house. "She put an ad in the university paper and said she'd pay for an hour's worth of work."

Mom trudges behind her, whispering through her teeth. "You make it sound so tawdry, Gloria!"

The truck is unloaded in less than ninety minutes with all the extra hands; the college guys even set up the beds for me and moved the furniture pieces into place. When they left at noon, they were carrying two pizzas Mom had ordered for them and a wad of cash. "I could have paid them, Mom," I say, unloading a box of glasses into a kitchen cupboard.

If I can get the kitchen set up, the beds made, and some clothes put into drawers, I'll feel great about today.

"Nonsense. I told you. This was my gift. This," she says, from the living room, "and a new sofa."

I can't see her but imagine her face pinched up into slight disgust. "We don't need a new sofa. That one's comfortable."

"Well then, I'll help with schooling for Ethan and Emma."

"They'll go to the public school, Mom. Taxes pay for that." I can hear her sigh. "Hey, Mom! Why don't you load up the kids and go get lunch for all of us?" She's trying so hard to be positive and not step on my toes or say something that upsets the children that she's driving me crazy. I'm relieved to get her out of the house for a while.

"She's worried," Gloria says. "The explosion and—" She turns to look at me.

"I know," I say, not letting her finish. I'm worried, too, but not in the sick-to-my-stomach way. I'm cautious or anxious; I don't know. I stopped believing a long time ago that life fits together like a jigsaw puzzle. The pieces are there; it just takes years,

a lifetime, or sometimes beyond that life before the pieces make sense. I'm just trying to put together the ones that fit today.

"For all her faults . . . and Lord knows she has a lot," Gloria says, making me smile, "deep down Miriam's a person."

I break down another box and lean against the counter. "I need to find a job, Gloria."

She stops and stands, grunting as she rises. "I know you do, babe, and I've already got the word out. The good news is people always need clean teeth."

"The bad news is the local dentists already have their hygienists. I'll have to look at the next town or two over."

Gloria wipes her forehead with her sleeve and small gray ringlets bob around her face. "Well, thankfully, people always get mad and quit or get fired or take a leave of absence to have a baby and then decide they don't want to work anymore. So let's hope somebody gets fired!"

I look around at everything that needs to be hooked together, like the TV and DVD player, the computer and printer, and all the stuff that goes with it to get Internet access. "I need my dad to come

help me with a lot of this stuff that I don't know how to do."

Gloria snaps her head up to look at me. "When's the last time Miriam's seen him?"

"My college graduation."

She laughs and swipes the hair out of her eyes. "That'll be good!"

I hadn't really thought of Dad and Mom seeing each other again when we decided to move to Grandon, but Dad *will* come visit the kids and me and Mom and Dad will be forced to be civil or hostile to each other. I can't think about that right now. All I know is that I need my dad.

We work until seven and my body is sore. I can't imagine how Mom and Gloria feel. Gloria looks as if she walked through a car wash, and Mom's honey-colored bob has been shoved behind her ears and her black slacks are sagging, ready for the dry cleaner. The kitchen is organized and Mom has stocked our fridge and freezer with food for the upcoming week.

The kids give big hugs good-bye and I help them find their pajamas in the drawers. "How long do we have to share a room?" Ethan asks, picking out his red jammies with the big football on the front.

"Until I don't know," I say, looking through Emma's chest of drawers.

"This room is too crowded," Emma says, balling up her blue jeans.

"Don't wad those up, please. Lay them at the end of your bed so you can wear them tomorrow." I pull a purple nightie over Emma's head and pull her long hair out of the neck hole. "This room isn't too crowded. You've got room for your beds and you each have a chest of drawers."

"There's no room for us to play," Emma says.

I sit on the edge of her bed and look at them. I am exhausted. "I think we're all tired and it's easy to be negative when you're tired. Let's eat some soup and call it a day."

The kids are overtired and I calm Emma down from a long crying jag at dinner. "I miss Daddy," she says, tears streaking her face. I cry along with her and hold her on my lap while she finishes eating.

When I put them to bed I run my thumb back and forth over each of their foreheads, trying to rub out or smooth away any worrying thoughts that are crowding their minds. We say our prayers—well, I say them for the kids because I know they're beyond tired at this point—but I pray out loud as they

snuggle deep into their blankets. I kiss them and fall
into my own bed after a quick shower; it feels like
my body is humming, still pulsing after a busy day.
These plain-as-cracker walls are so empty. Kyle always helped hang pictures. If left to me, these walls
might be forever barren. I see the box marked "bedroom photos" and sit on the edge of the bed, opening it. I remove the newspaper wrapped around two
framed photos of Ethan and Emma's baby pictures
and I set them on the dresser. I unwrap the next
frame and it's a picture of Kyle and me at Niagara
Falls before we had the kids. He's holding me from
behind, resting his chin on my shoulder because I'm
so short. I smile, looking at him: so handsome with
his thick, brown hair and sharp green eyes. "I miss
you," I say, tapping the picture.

Although it's late, I pick up my cell phone off the
nightstand and check one final time for texts and
e-mails. I need to call the phone company tomorrow
to get us hooked up with Internet and phone service
ASAP so I can set up the computer. I spend an hour
writing an e-mail because it takes me forever on the
tiny cell phone pad. The muffled sounds of yelling
creep through my walls, and I set the phone on my
nightstand, listening. Our neighbor is shouting, but

it seems to be one-sided, into the phone no doubt. I lie down and stare up at the ceiling, holding Kyle's picture to my chest and waiting for her to hang up so I can get some sleep. The shouting ends and I wonder what she's doing over there now? Pacing the floor? Raiding the refrigerator? Breaking something? It's all part of the process. I know it well. Now I'm just tired and praying and thinking of Kyle and waiting for tomorrow.

Two

I've learned from experience that the greater part of our happiness or misery depends on our dispositions and not on our circumstances.
—MARTHA WASHINGTON

GRETCHEN

I wake up early and begin to unload boxes of clothes into my drawers and closet. I'll work in here as long as I can so I don't wake up the kids. They begin school on Monday and I want them to be rested. At eight o'clock, I'm inside my small bathroom organizing my cabinets when I hear the soft padding of feet across the carpeted floor. Emma stands in the doorway with Sugar in her arms and eyes half cracked from heavy sleep. Her hair is blond like mine and hangs at the side of her face, tangled like

13

fishing line. "It smells kind of funny here," she says, stretching.

"That's a new smell," I say, emptying out the final box and breaking it down. "New carpet, new glue, new paint."

"So it's fancy?" she says, trying to fit inside one of the bigger boxes.

I laugh and motion for her to get out of the box. I know full well the construction is cheap; the builder cut costs wherever he could, including these thin-as-cardboard cabinets, but it's home. When Kyle would come home after a tour of duty, he would hold his tongue when someone complained about their house, job, the heat, or potholes in the road. He would have just come from sleeping on a cot, brushing his teeth outside with sand beneath his feet, driving on a road that was more holes than dirt, with hidden bombs along the way, and holding his position in one-hundred-plus degrees of heat, wearing long sleeves and carrying a rifle. He didn't have much tolerance for someone when they complained that their coffee was cold.

"Sure! Let's think of it as fancy," I say. Emma leads us into the hallway, and I can see Ethan digging through a box in their bedroom.

"Whatcha looking for?" I ask, leaning my head inside the door.

"My connecting pieces I build stuff out of." He's so much like his dad. He loves to put things together: a model airplane, a Radio Flyer wagon, a block castle just for the challenge. He's in heaven if something can be dismantled and then put back together again, whereas I cringe at the thought of Lincoln Logs or LEGOs.

"Just empty out that box and I'll take it out to the curb along with these others, and then we'll eat breakfast." Ethan brings the box to me as I'm coming back in for another load. A gust of early winter wind blows in, and I hurry as I pick up several more of the boxes that I've flattened. Ethan grabs a few and stumbles out the door behind me. Emma chooses to watch us from the warmth of the entryway. My pajama bottoms and T-shirt are too flimsy for this wind and I hurry, stacking the boxes at the curb. A rolling sound makes me look up and I see our neighbor, Mary Sunshine, pulling her garbage can down the driveway. I attempt a half smile, embarrassed to be out here in my pajamas, and if she smiles, I don't recognize it. Perhaps people smile differently here; maybe their mouths look frozen in a perpetual scowl.

"We have garbage, too," Ethan says, dumping his boxes onto the stack. She bobs her head in what I guess is a nod. "Bet we'll end up having more garbage than anybody on the whole street today." The revelation sinks into the competitive part of his brain and he glances down the street. "Yep. Just look. Nobody has higher garbage."

"And we're not even done bringing it all out yet," I say, more to Ethan than to her, whatever she said her name was.

"Are you going to work?" Ethan asks.

"Yes," she says, slapping the garbage handle grime off her hands and walking up her driveway.

"My dad had a bad accident on his job. A bomb went off and he—"

I don't want to talk about this so early in the morning. I fold my arms against the winds and take quick steps toward Ethan. "Let's go get some more boxes and see how high that stack can get." I look at her. "Have a great day at work." The look on her face is a smile, frown, grimace—what in the world do you call that kind of expression? Ethan and I finish hauling out the boxes, and he gives me a high five when we discover that yes, we do have more garbage than anyone else on the street.

Emma is tilted back on her heels, holding on to the doors of an open cabinet, and I imagine the entire cupboard coming loose from the wall. "Don't swing on the cabinets, Em."

"Why not? I'm hungry."

I open one of the bottom cabinets, revealing the few boxes of cereal we have: Cheerios, Rice Krispies, and Frosted Mini-Wheats. "Ta-da!"

"Where's the fun cereal?"

"This is it," I say, reaching for the Rice Krispies. "Ta-da always means *whoo hoo!* Look at this! Nothing says fun like snap, crackle, and pop." I pick up the boxes of cereal and give each of them a shake. There's hardly any Frosted Mini-Wheats left, and I wonder why I packed the box in the first place. Kyle wouldn't have packed it. Army men pride themselves on their packing skills! "Kyle, you need to go through these cupboards," I say to myself, throwing away the empty box. I'm feeling sorry for myself again and I hear Kyle's voice telling me to push myself up out of the rubble.

He grew up in Oklahoma, and when he was ten a tornado swept through his small town in the early morning hours. Kyle and his parents and brother leaped from their beds, his mother in her nightgown

and the men of the house in their underwear, and ran to the cellar as the twister tore off the roof of their home. When the winds died down and his father cracked open the cellar door, the sky was jagged with splintered trees and their truck was missing along with the living room and Kyle's bedroom. The henhouse was razed and the chickens stripped of feathers and lying dead, but the barn was standing so they walked toward it to check on the horses. Kyle heard a noise, something like scratching, and stepped toward the boards of the henhouse. He yelled for his family, and each of them stepped closer, listening for the sound. As the sun rose, the noise became more frantic and they watched as the featherless head of the rooster pushed his way through the boards. He lifted his naked body from the rubble and stumbled to the top of the boards, crowing with what strength he had left.

Kyle told that story several times in our marriage. "He had to crow," Kyle always said. "It was in his DNA."

One night during my senior year in high school, I was driving home from a waitressing job and was pulled over for speeding. The officer flashed his light in my face and the streetlight illuminated him. I tried

not to smile but couldn't help it. He took my license and car registration to his vehicle and was gone for just a minute, not long enough to issue a ticket, when he walked back to the car and let me go. "Slow down, Gretchen," he said, making me smile.

Days later I was at a pancake house eating with a friend when a yummy-looking guy walked in wearing jeans and a short-sleeved shirt, and I thought he looked familiar but couldn't place him. He walked to the table, and when I looked up at him, just as I'd done out my car window a few nights earlier, I recognized him. "Taking it slower?" he asked. I laughed and felt so high schoolish but realized a guy his age (he looked twenty-something) wouldn't be interested in me. He sat with us and we all talked for two hours, but I still didn't think he liked me. He was seven years older than me, five years with the police department, and he'd just joined the army. Somehow, I knew that was in his DNA. He was born to help and protect. You just know that about some people. I never saw myself as an army wife, but when Kyle and I started dating I suddenly couldn't see myself being anything else. We married after I graduated from college. My parents were adamant that I wait. I think they fully expected Kyle to lose

interest, but he didn't. Kyle had been in the army four years when we married; he wore his dress blues at our wedding and we began hanging a sign outside the door of our home at each military post that said, HOME IS WHEREVER THE ARMY SENDS YOU! The sign is hanging in my new kitchen now. I just couldn't get rid of it.

Ethan and Em are chattering away over their bowls when I hear a knock at the door. A sweatshirt is crumpled on the sofa, and I slip it over my head before reaching for the door. A man's bald head is all I can see through the peephole and I open the door. He's fiftyish, I guess, with dark bags under his eyes and heavy lines on each side of his mouth. He looks cold and aggravated. "Hi," I say, making it sound more like a question than a greeting.

"Sorry to bother you so early," he says, pulling his coat collar up to cover his neck. "I'm looking for Ramona's daughter."

"Nope. I'm Miriam's daughter," I say, smiling.

His chest deflates, pushing a huge gust of air out of his mouth. "Do you know Ramona?"

"I've never heard of her. I'm brand-new here as of yesterday."

He looks behind him, at what I don't know.

"Great!" He scratches his head and sighs again. "I need to find Ramona's daughter. Another tenant in my building said she lives on this street, but he couldn't remember her name and I can't either."

I cross my arms to keep warm. "I have no idea. Did he say if she's married or has children? That could narrow it down."

"She's single."

"I think the woman who lives on the other side of me is single, but I'm not sure. I can't even remember her name."

"Her name's Melissa," Ethan says, wedging in next to me.

"That's her!" the man says. "Ramona's daughter is Melissa."

"Then that's her place," I say. He turns to step off the porch. "She's not home right now. I saw her leave a few minutes ago."

If it's even possible, his chest shrinks even more. "Do you know how to contact her?" I shake my head. "Okay, this has been a"—he sees Ethan and stops—"rotten morning. When she gets home, would you tell her that her mom died and I need her to come clean out her mom's place?"

Ethan snaps his head to look up at me, and I feel

letters burbling up, but none of them are coming out as words. "What? No! I only met her for the first time yesterday. Don't the police make that sort of notification?"

"The police came late last night when Ramona wouldn't answer her phone. The old dame's hand turned the stereo up blasting loud when she keeled over and died. Had every tenant calling me to take care of it. She wouldn't answer the phone or the door so the police went in and found her."

"So why can't they notify her daughter?"

He popped a cigarette into his mouth like it was an M&M. "I told you," he says, lighting the cigarette and puffing. "Nobody knows Ramona's kid. Hard to contact next of kin when the dead woman never said she had kin. If I hadn't heard them screaming at each other a few times I wouldn't even know it." He turns to leave. "Tell her I'm giving her one week to go through her mother's things and then I'm dumping all of it."

"I'm not going to tell her," I say to his back.

He turns to look at me. "Tell her I'm being nice. I could just rummage through that junk and keep what I like."

I nudge Ethan to get back into the house and I stand out on the porch, closing the door. "I can't tell her that. You need to leave a note on her door."

He won't turn back to look at me. "I've been out here for an hour knocking on doors." He tosses his hand in the air. "I'm done."

Ethan is staring up at me when I step back inside. "Who was that guy, Mom?"

"A landlord," I say, busying myself by putting away the cereal.

He picks up his football and tosses it from hand to hand. "Who died?"

Emma looks up from her soggy bowl of cereal, frightened. "Somebody died? Who died?"

I cross to her and kiss her head. "Our neighbor's mom."

"Oh." Ethan tosses the ball up and down now, and I try to ignore it as I go back to work in the kitchen. I'm not in the mood for the whole football-in-the-house argument. "You don't like her very much, do you, Mom?"

Great! Caught not liking someone by my own child! I stop my work to look at him. "What makes you say that? She seems fine."

He tosses that confounded ball higher into the air. "You don't talk as much to her as you do other people."

"I just don't know her very well yet."

The ball goes up again. "You talk long with other strangers."

"Please take that ball out of the house, Ethan." He tosses it back and forth all the way to the front door before tossing it out into the yard.

All the big kitchen items have a cupboard to call their own, but the counter space is littered with things that will eventually wind up crammed into a drawer or shoe box: rubber bands, pens, old address book, two small picture frames, sticky pads, cow-shaped eraser, handful of magnets, Magic Markers, a whistle, two batteries, a tube of ChapStick, a purse-size package of tissues, a ruler, and a stack of cards we received after Kyle's accident. I fan them out in my hand, not knowing what to do with them. I see a small, empty box and stack them in a corner of it, pushing the rest of the stuff from the counter on top of them. I sigh, setting the box on the table. There's so much to do, but I know Kyle's accident and the move have been a lot to take in for the kids. I wander through the hall to their bedroom and peek

inside. Emma is using one of her baby blankets to make a bed for Sugar, and Ethan is pulling children's books out of a box.

Whenever Kyle was home the kids would beg him to read to them every night at bedtime. I always read using inflection and different, even if sometimes weak, voices, but Kyle had a certain flair when he "read" *Charlotte's Web* or *Goldilocks and the Three Bears*. In Kyle's translation, Charlotte the spider spun the words *armpit, nose hair,* and *burp* into her web. Ethan and Emma especially liked *burp* because Wilbur the pig then walked through the barnyard belching. For *Goldilocks and the Three Bears,* I could hear Ethan's high-pitched belly laugh as Kyle read, "Then Mama Bear said, 'Somebody's been pooting on my chair,' and then little Baby Bear said, 'Somebody's been pooting on my chair and blew a hole right through it!'" It didn't matter how many times Kyle read that story, the kids would howl like it was a brand-new telling. I watch the kids and pray. I've never prayed so much in my life. I wash the dishes and pray. I fold laundry and pray. I shower and cook and scrub the floor and pray. It keeps me tethered, grounded, buoyed, or from going insane.

I hang on to their door as I stick my head into

their room. "Hey! Do either of you know where the box of games is? We could play something."

"Right now?" Emma asks, pushing Sugar's head hard into the blanket.

"Sure."

"I thought you were busy," Ethan says.

I step into their room. "Why don't we get the books and games and everything put away in your room and then it will be totally done! That should only take a few minutes. Then let's play a game." I feel the crush of things to do, but know I need to spend time with them.

We finish their room and we celebrate by playing two games of Candy Land and then one of Sorry! and then Battleship with Emma before Mom picks them up to take to her house to eat lunch and spend the rest of the day. Hopefully, by the time they make it home tomorrow I'll have most everything in order. "Are you sure you don't want me to stay and help you?" Mom asks.

"You are helping by giving the kids a break from tripping over of all this stuff," I say, waving my arm into the living room. "Hopefully, I'll find a spot for all of it." I kiss Emma and Ethan and resist asking them to stay with me so I can see them, touch them,

and hear their voices. My throat tightens as I wave to them from the front door.

I haul out the final empty boxes from the kids' room and feel good that their bedroom is organized. I make a quick trip to the school to take the kid's shot records and fill out the rest of the enrollment papers and then spend the rest of the day working in my bedroom and organizing the linen and laundry closets. I walk through the condo and know I need to put up some Christmas decorations soon. The sight of lights, evergreen swags, stars, bulbs, the tree, and nativity will make all of us feel better. The first Christmas after my parents divorced I hated putting up the tree and dragging out the nativity, but once they were up, my feelings changed. I search for the boxes filled with all things Christmas so the kids and I can start decorating in the next few days.

The stack of flattened boxes is growing at the front door, and I start to take them out when I see the neighbor's car pull into her driveway, so I close the door before she sees me. Through the window sheers I can see her walking to her mailbox. I set the boxes down. I'm not going to the curb now. If I see her, I'll wonder if anyone has told her about her mother and then be plagued with guilt that I didn't

tell her. I shake my head. What a preposterous situation!

This place is too quiet without the kids. I fall into bed and dial Mom's number to say good night to them but discover they're too busy to come to the phone. "They're distracted," Mom says. I smile. She's always been very distracting, and right now that's a good thing. I hang up and stare at the ceiling, thinking of my neighbor. Kyle would have told her her mother had died. Even if his world had collapsed in on him, Kyle would have pushed his way up through the rubble and done what he was supposed to do.

"Someone has to tell her," he'd say. "If the landlord is a coward, then someone needs to step up." Kyle would get out of bed at this very moment and go knock on her door, but I turn the light off and pull the blankets up to my neck.

Three

It is dismal coming home, when there is nobody to
welcome one!
—Ann Radcliffe

MELISSA

I never knew my father, but when one of Ramona's
men traipsed through our apartment late at night
I'd tiptoe out to the living room, kitchen, or her bedroom where I could see them drinking, smoking,
or dancing while each of them held on to a bottle
of Jack. I'd imagine which, if any, of those nightly
visitors was my father. I asked Ramona one time
who my father was, and she slapped me across the
face. "It's none of your business," she said, her ran-
cid liquor breath burning my eyes. "The only thing
he ever did was plant the seed of a fool." It took me

years to realize that seed was me. She has gone out of her way to let people know she doesn't have children, least of all a daughter, the most worthless of seed. The fact that I live less than three miles from Ramona is ironic to the point of being absurd. We lived in Florida for as long as I could remember. Ten years ago, out of loyalty or extreme stupidity, I followed her here to Grandon, where the winds are as cold in winter as Ramona was on any given day. We talk when she needs money, and the sick, crippled part of me actually wants to help her, while the other part loathes her whiskey voice and the sight of her swollen, overliquored face. She called two nights ago and asked for a hundred bucks to "see her through," calling me "baby girl" and "lamby," the names she's always called me after she's cussed me or slapped my face until it welted in stripes. "Don't leave me, baby girl," she'd say when I was a child. "What would Mommy do without her lamby?" When I refused to give the money to her two nights ago she called me every four-letter word in the book and I reciprocated. I learned how to do combat with her years ago.

This condo is as barren as I am: white, empty walls, cheap carpet, and tacky furniture. It's a re-

flection of me and I hate it. I groaned when I saw the moving truck next door and two small children running through the yard, their high-pitched voices slipping through the cracks in my windowsills. I work two jobs to pay my bills and I don't have the time or the interest in "learning more" about my neighbors. They've lived there two days and already the mother has a Christmas wreath on the front door. The condo on the other side of me, owned by an older husband and wife, is bloated with Christmas decorations: lights, wreaths, evergreen swags, nativity set, and two reindeer that move their heads as if they're eating. My condo is the thorn between two roses. I've never owned a Christmas wreath or put up a Christmas tree. What's the point when you live alone? I was married once; it lasted almost two years, an eternity really, considering neither of us was fit for marriage.

As I pull out of the garage I see my new neighbor draping Christmas lights over the miserly shrubs in front of her condo with the phone pressed to her ear. That's the second time I've seen her wandering in the cold, talking on the phone. From the corner of my eye I can tell she's watching me pull away, probably

hoping for a moment of witty banter between us or to invite me in to their warm, smells-like-pumpkin-bread home that's already fully decorated for Christmas. I dislike her already, and I can't even remember her name.

I've worked in the mail room of Wilson's Department Store during the morning hours for two years now. It's only part-time work, so I transfer hard copy files on to the computer for Layton and Associates, a small law office, in the afternoon. In the same sense, I take the latest cases, which are on computer and make a hard copy file for each one. Feels like they're doubling up on their work, but hey, they're paying me to do it, so I don't complain. Both jobs are what Ramona calls "grunt work," perfect for grunts like me, she says. Before that, I worked on the assembly line at the pencil factory. You'd be surprised how many pencils don't make the cut and get pitched into a huge trash barrel. I do my jobs and go home. How I learned to work is beyond me because Ramona couldn't hold a thought in her head let alone a job. She'd been a cashier, gas station attendant, waitress, prep cook, night janitor, and Avon Lady all in the same year. "I change jobs like I change men," she said to me once, all boozed up and proud. I pay my

bills. I stay out of the way. I probably drink too much, although I've always said I'd never be like Ramona. I'd cut my right hand off before I turned into her.

Robert Layton is a good twenty-plus years older than me, but I think he's good-looking with the lines shooting out toward his temples and curving the sides of his mouth. He's not slobby; he hasn't let himself go like some older guys you see. I guess he's a good lawyer because his office is busy, with Jodi and Susan turning more people away than taking them on as clients. Robert's a grandfather and doesn't run, in his words, the hamster wheel anymore. I don't pal around with Jodi and Susan, the other women in the office, and when Robert invites the staff over to his house on the Fourth of July and for the annual Christmas dinner, I never go. The file room is at the back of the office and I'm always in there alone so I'd feel out of my skin if I was plopped down at a dinner party next to Jodi or Robert's wife, Kate.

I finish work earlier than usual because it always slows down around the holidays at Robert's office, and I sit in my car, letting it warm up. Snow is falling, but it looks like it's in slow motion, the flakes are

so big and puffy. I watch a woman who looks like my mother—hunched shoulders, thick in the middle, and short legs—walk across the square. She's holding the hand of a small child and heading into Wilson's to buy a Christmas gift for the child's mother, no doubt. I've always felt as if there were two women inside me: one who is desperate, drowning, and clinging to anything that can float and the other woman who feels the depth of loss and the hope of beauty and is always searching for the marvelous to spring up out of the gray. That woman rarely shows up, it seems. There's no need to sift through my emotions right now; the image of the grandmother and child leaves me with a drowning feeling in my stomach, so I drive away.

The little boy next door is tossing a football into the air and catching it when I approach the condo. He waves and I ignore him, pretending not to see as my garage door opens and I pull inside, shutting the garage door behind me before he can run over and tell me all the inane parts of his day. I feel at some point that I should ask what happened to his father, but something inside me doesn't want to know. I prefer this in-between existence, where I know very little and have to give little in return.

I'm eating a bowl of canned soup and watching TV when someone knocks on the front door. I try to ignore it but realize the light from the TV shines out the front window, giving me away. I step to the door and see the mother from next door through the peephole. She probably wants to borrow something, like a screwdriver I'll never be able to find or a hammer I've never owned. I open the door a few inches and look out at her face. She's around my age, I suspect, but she looks younger. She's taken better care of herself. She's blond and petite to my blah-brown hair and lanky torso. "Hi," she says. "I'm Gretchen from next door. Remember?" I look at her as if that was a stupid thing to say and her face registers that she agrees. She's cold and wraps her arms around her. The little boy and girl come running up behind her, and she turns in a huff. "Go back home and stay inside like I asked."

"But what are you doing?" the little girl asks.

I feel myself getting irritated. It's cold and I want to close the door.

"I'll be right back," Gretchen says. "Go inside and get your pajamas on like I asked. Take your brother back inside." The girl grabs the little boy's hand and jerks him toward her. "Sorry," the woman

says, looking sheepishly at me. "I . . . a man knocked on my door yesterday morning looking for you and . . ." She pulls her sweater tighter around her and looks out toward the empty street. "I told him that you lived here, but he said he wasn't going to come back."

This is going to take forever. "Who was it?"

"I don't know his name. He didn't say. He's the landlord at the apartments where your mother—"

"What about him?" I'm abrupt and she looks startled.

"He said that he found your mother . . ."

Stand still. Don't react. Ramona did this to herself. It doesn't involve you.

"She died in her apartment, and he said he'd like you to clean out her place or else he will."

I nod. "Thanks."

She catches the door before I can close it. "I'm sorry about your mother."

"I'm not," I say, leaving her in the cold.

I walk back to the sofa and sit down, staring at the TV screen. What am I watching? Today's Friday. When did she say Ramona died? The landlord came yesterday morning. When did she die? Wasn't it just two days ago that I talked to her? She asked for

money and called me a worthless pig. That's how sixty years ended. She yelled, she took, she misused, she swore, she badgered, she abused, and then her eyes closed and her mouth shut. I'm glad it's over. That sliver of me that always wanted something, anything from Ramona, will have to find something else to covet now. I turn off the TV and sit in the dark, waiting for morning.

Four

*We make our friends; we make our enemies; but
God makes our next-door neighbor.*
—G. K. CHESTERTON

GRETCHEN

Ethan's chatter wakes me up way too early. His
voice has always had a way of drilling through
hardwoods and mortar. It took me half the night to
fall asleep. I tossed and turned, thinking about the
look on Melissa's face when I told her her mother
was dead. Shouldn't there have been something—a
short, quick gasp, a sigh, a twitch, even a nervous
laugh? Who doesn't have some sort of emotion when
a parent dies? I replay her closing the door on my
face as I make pancakes for the kids and feel the ir-
ritation burrowing beneath my skin. But what's

irritating me? The fact that she doesn't care that her mother died or that I took so long to tell her? Kyle was right. I overthink things. While the kids are playing, I check my e-mail and find myself getting teary-eyed reading them. There are several from Kyle's parents, Tom and Alice, who attach several pictures of Kyle to each e-mail with a detailed description of when the photo was taken. I dry my eyes before the kids can see me and send an e-mail, attaching a few photos of our new home and the kids before making breakfast.

Ethan is eating his pancakes before I have time to put syrup on them. "Are we going to that lady's funeral?" he asks.

"What lady?" I realize who he means as the question crosses the air between us. "Oh. No, we're not."

"Why not?"

I pour syrup over each of their pancakes and then my own. "Because we never knew her."

"We got lots of cards and flowers and stuff from people we don't know," Emma says.

"I know but . . ."

"That's what we should do, Mom," Ethan says, his mouth too full to talk. "We should make her a card and send her flowers."

I take a bite and realize that my kids are better people than I am. "You're right. That's what we need to do." I don't want to; I envision Melissa crushing the flowers in her hand like a cookie and torching the card by breathing on it.

They dig out a piece of blue construction paper and work on the card together after breakfast, and by the time I have cleaned the kitchen, the paper is covered in flowers with bloated, misshaped petals and a rainbow dripping glittery glue streaks. "We'll let it dry and a little later we'll go out for some flowers."

"Let's go now, and by the time we get back, the card will be dry," Emma says.

I don't want to go now. "Why don't we get some things done and then we'll make a trip out?"

"What's left to do?" Ethan asks. "We already unpacked everything."

"Yes, we did, didn't *we*?" I say. It's no use. They'll just keep asking and wear me down. "Get your clothes on and let's go."

As we back out of the driveway I'm already planning what to say to Melissa this time. Maybe when she opens the door she'll sock me in the eye or twist my arm behind my back or take the flowers out of

my hand and clunk them over my head. None of the scenarios are looking good. I know I can't really afford a bouquet from the florist, so I pull into the grocery store for one there. "All I have to do is tie a ribbon around this and it will look just like we bought it from a florist," I say, picking up a small glass vase.

"Can she dry these?" Emma asks, holding a small bouquet.

I look at the flowers. "No, not really. These aren't good ones for drying."

"Then we need to get ones she can dry." She looks up at me. "Like you did with all our flowers."

"But those flowers were for your dad and . . . I don't think Melissa was very close to her mom, so I don't think these flowers are going to mean as much as—" They're both looking at me. I set the flowers back in the container and pull out a bunch with more roses in it. "These will dry much better."

The card is still tacky when we get home, and it takes me far too long to convince the kids that we really should wait for it to dry before we deliver it. Part of me just wants to get it over with, but the other part clearly wants to put this off until Emma's college graduation. I spend the greater part of the morning on the phone while the kids play, and when

I'm finishing the last conversation with Kyle's parents, both Em and Ethan are staring at me and patting their bellies. We eat sandwiches and chips, and I dread one of them bringing up the card and flowers. To my surprise and delight they both forget and run back to their room to continue playing, when Ethan yells from the hall, "Hey! What about our card, Mom? When are we taking it over?"

"Right now," I say, as if I had it planned all along. I make the kids put on their coats or else we'll just stand out on Melissa's porch looking like those toy monkeys with the chattering teeth and clanging cymbals. Ethan is the first to her door and knocks on it, way too loud to be polite, and I stop his hand from knocking again. I groan when I hear footsteps and put on a pleasant, barely-there smile when I know Melissa's looking at us through the peephole. The door opens and Ethan shoves the card through the slim opening.

"We made this for you," he says, propping his fisted hands onto his hips.

"Thanks," Melissa says, glancing at the card.

I work hard at a smile but feel awkward.

"We got these for you, too," Emma says, handing her the vase full of flowers.

"Thanks."

All four of us stand in gangly silence before she says thanks again. "Okay, come on, kids," I say, turning them back to our house. The door closes before I can even get the kids off the porch, and it takes all the willpower I have not to say something ugly. "There," I say, opening our door. "That was a nice thing to do, and the flowers and card will be just the things to make her home a little happier." I doubted this completely, but it sounded convincing enough so that the kids ran back to whatever they had been playing in their room.

When Mom drops by later in the afternoon she is carrying a big pot. Mom doesn't cook; she never did. My father did most of the cooking when they were married, but when it was up to Mom we mostly ate a lot of canned soups, boxed rice dishes, and noodle dinners. Mom's third and final husband, Len, was a great cook. I still miss his sweet potato bread pudding he made every Thanksgiving. Len was a great fit for my mother, whereas she and Dad could rub each other the wrong way without even being in the same room. It wasn't always that way. I remember them being happy together. I don't know how things went south in their marriage.

"I didn't make this," Mom says, reading my face. "Gloria made a huge pot of chicken and dumplings for you and the children." I step forward to take it from her. "I did make a salad, though, along with a batch of chocolate chip cookies."

"You made cookies?"

She stops on the sidewalk and turns back to me. "I have learned to make some things over the years." Her red silk scarf blows in the wind as she reaches inside her car. "Since Gloria insists on serving cookies to the children at Glory's Place she also insisted that I learn how to make them." She steps inside and looks around. "Look at this! You are all put together."

"Still odds and ends that don't have a place, but most of it's put away," I say, taking the cookies and salad from her.

The kids tackle Mom when they hear her voice and drag her by the hand to their room. I lift the lid of the pot and breathe it in; I haven't had chicken and dumplings in ages. I yell for the kids and Mom to wash up as I gather some plates. Kyle always complained that I didn't make chicken and dumplings enough. "They take so much time," I always said to him. If he was here today I'd double the recipe so

he'd have chicken and dumplings for days. As I scoop it onto the plates I wonder if I had ever made it for him at all?

"We bought flowers for the woman who died," Ethan says, taking a seat next to Mom.

"What woman who died?"

I shake my head, filling Ethan's plate with food. "A man showed up here and said the mother of the woman next to us died and that I had to break the news to her."

"I've never heard of such a thing."

I laugh. "Yeah. Neither did I, and I told him I wouldn't do it."

"So he told her and you bought her flowers?"

"No, he didn't tell her. Kyle told her." Mom glances up at me. "His voice kept nagging me . . . so I did it."

"What an awful way to break the ice. Was she just devastated?"

"I wouldn't say that," I say, choosing my words. "The guy has given her a few days to clean out her mom's place, but I don't think she's going to do it."

"I'd clean your house out if you died," Emma says. Mom and I both laugh. "And I'd take every single picture of you and Dad and Sugar and the toy box Dad made me."

"What about my stuff?" Ethan says. "What about my plastic soldiers and all my animals?"

"I don't want those things," Em says.

Ethan opens his mouth to fight about the soldiers and fluffy lambs when I stop them. "Hey! I'm not dead." They both look at me with fallen, flat faces. I laugh and point to their food. "This is delicious!"

Mom dips another helping of chicken and dumplings onto her plate. "Well, there must be something in her mother's place that she'd want. Surely, she doesn't want a complete stranger rifling through her memories."

"Yeah," Ethan says. "I wouldn't want some stranger touching my soldiers!"

"Nobody would want your soldiers!" Emma says.

"I want 'em! Dad gave them to me." Mom distracts the kids with the story of the time she took my brother and me to the zoo and I thought it'd be a good idea if we just left him there. Em thinks that is especially funny.

Mom plays a card game in the living room with the kids as I put our plates in the dishwasher and work at finding something for the leftovers. "There's enough food here for twenty," I say, looking for bowls

I hope will be a good fit. I find two bowls and pour the chicken and dumplings inside them, thinking. Why was that blasted woman next door making me wrestle so much? I toss some cookies into a plastic bag, pick up one of the bowls, and walk over to the card game in the middle of the living-room floor. "Be right back," I say, before any of them can question me. I knock on Melissa's door and decide I'll just leave everything sitting here if she doesn't answer. It's dark on the porch and inside her home; her place doesn't even *feel* like Christmas! When she opens the door I can see from the streetlight that her face is puffy and her eyes are small. "We had extra food," I say, keeping it short. "A friend made it. It's delicious."

She opens the door a bit and reaches for it. "Thanks."

I turn to leave but look at her over my shoulder. "I can go with you if you want." Her face is blank. I don't know why I suggested such a thing, but I'm still blabbing away. "I can help you clean out your mom's place."

"I'm not going to."

"I know. But . . . one day you might really regret

that . . . letting a stranger go through her stuff." She opens her mouth and I plow ahead. "There may be something there that you didn't know about or had forgotten about or something you want to give to somebody." She is shaking her head, and the air is sitting on my cheeks, hurting them. "You can let me know. The kids start school on Monday and I can go then, or my mom can watch them if you want to go tomorrow."

"I don't want to go."

"All right," I say, stepping off the porch, relieved she doesn't want to do it. "If you change your mind, you know where I am."

I shiver going through the door and plop down on the sofa. "Where'd you go?" Mom asks, shuffling the cards.

"Tried to deliver some Christmas cheer."

"And how'd that go?"

"People make it hard," I say, picking up the cards Mom is dealing for Go Fish.

"Well, you know, I've always been a very good judge of people," Mom says, organizing the cards in her hand. "That's why I like so very few of them."

I laugh out loud and look at the kids. "She doesn't mean that."

"I wasn't even listening," Emma says.

Mom rears her head back and cackles. I organize my cards and realize I've been dealt a bum hand. That's how it goes sometimes.

Five

Grief can't be shared. Everyone carries it alone.
His own burden in his own way.

—ANNE MORROW LINDBERGH

MELISSA

I never went to bed but stayed on the couch watching mindless television. I wondered if Ramona died in her bed or while watching TV on the sofa, or was she about to leave her apartment when death came for her? I wondered if it was snowing out when she died and if she was standing at the window watching it fall? I wondered, too, if the man who was my father would even remember her or care that she was dead? He wouldn't, I say aloud to no one. I don't care, so why would he? I ate some of the chicken and dumplings at one in the morning. I can't remem-

ber the last time I've had something that good. When I was seven or eight, Ramona and I lived next to the Schweigers, a family whose apartment always smelled like a bakery. Mrs. Schweiger was Hungarian or something; I don't remember, but I loved her accent. She invited me over a lot for dinner, and years later I wondered if she suspected that I didn't eat much at my place. "Would your mother like to come, too?" she'd say, looking over my head for anyone who might be supervising me.

"She's not here," I said every time. Most of the time it was true, but sometimes Ramona would be inside the apartment, passed out on the sofa or sleeping with the man of the hour. The Schweigers ate every meal together: bacon and eggs, pancakes, meatloaf and mashed potatoes, baked chicken, scalloped potatoes, or spaghetti with meatballs, and there was always dessert. Karla was fifteen when I met them, Madden was twelve, and Louie was eight. I played with Louie every day. Sometimes I fell asleep on their couch and Mrs. Schweiger would leave me there. She'd knock on Ramona's door, and if Ramona wasn't there she'd leave a note on the door, letting her know I was with them.

The Schweigers took me to church every Sunday.

I remember the first time Mrs. Schweiger asked if I wanted to go with them. I shrugged and said sure. I'd never been inside a church before, but if it meant being with the Schweigers, I was all for it. There was nothing complicated about the Schweigers' faith; it was dirt plain and natural. When I remember Mrs. Schweiger I realize she never talked about religion. She talked about God and Jesus like they were part of the family. I spent three Christmases with the Schweigers. Ramona and some sidewalk Santa Claus spent one Christmas together at his apartment, and I don't remember where she was for the other two Christmases I spent inside the Schweigers' apartment, opening presents, like a baby doll and a purse, that I never expected.

"I know what God is like, Mrs. Schweiger," I said on that Christmas Day, watching her peel potatoes.

"What is he like?" she asked, throwing the peels into the garbage.

"He's like you."

She stopped her work and looked at me. She knelt down and held my face, kissing my forehead: I could feel her wet potato hands on my cheeks. "Believe it or not, God loves you even more than I do, Melissy," she'd say. She always called me Melissy,

and I was surprised at how much I liked that. I loved being loved by Mrs. Schweiger.

Louie and I played with Bruce Linton from upstairs, a kid four years younger than me who always had a snotty nose. Every day in the winter his sleeve was crusty with dried snot. If things didn't go Bruce's way, he'd slap or kick Louie and me, but we were both bigger and could pin him down until he stopped acting like a baby. Bruce also ate dinner a lot at the Schweigers' but not because his parents weren't around. Many times his parents ate with us, too. Playing with Louie and Bruce and being with the Schweigers was the best three years of my life, and I gushed like Niagara on the day we moved away.

"I've prayed for you, Melissy," Mrs. Schweiger said on that final day. "And I'll keep praying, okay?" I nodded, not really believing in it too much because I prayed that we wouldn't ever, ever move away from the Schweigers, but Ramona got a wild hair and loaded us into the station wagon. "Don't ever stop praying," Mrs. Schweiger said, her eyes wet and drippy. "Don't ever stop believing." Tears streaked my face as we pulled away, my arm flapping in the air. I think what little belief I had ended that day on those two hundred miles to Jacksonville.

To my knowledge, Ramona never really talked to Mrs. Schweiger beyond that occasional cracked apartment door. Ramona made it a point to never know anyone at any of the places we lived; it made running out in the middle of the night so much easier. She cheated landlords out of a lot of money but always waved it off, saying, "It will cost them more to track us down than what we owe them."

I warm up another plate of chicken and dumplings for lunch and hear someone talking outside the front window. Moving the blinds, I see Gretchen on the phone again. Talking to her boyfriend, no doubt, a man the kids don't necessarily like but someone she can't break things off with, not yet, anyway. I sit on the sofa and eat, watching her through the blinds. The conversation is serious. She hasn't smiled yet but keeps pushing her hair behind her ear and looking at the front door of her home. I finish eating and step to the window, watching. She takes the phone from her ear and crosses toward her door. I open mine and pretend to see her. "Oh. Hi."

"Hi," she says, waving at me with the phone.

"Those chicken and dumplings were really good."

"My mom's friend made them."

I step out and look at her. I'm just standing here,

and she feels uncomfortable, I can tell. I clear my throat and take a breath. "I don't know how long it will take to clean out Ramona's apartment . . . so if you can't, it's no big deal. I thought it might go fast if two . . . .she had a lot of junk mostly, so it shouldn't take too long."

"Sure," she says, thumping the phone against her thigh. "When?"

"I work until five each day so . . ." I fade out and look at a passing car.

"Do you want to go today?"

I wasn't expecting this, to do it so soon. "Could you?"

"I'll call my mom and see if she can come over to be with the kids."

I close the door and feel my heart racing. Why was I doing this? Why do I even care what's in the middle of Ramona's pile of rubble? Anger at what I just did makes me flush with heat, and I fan my shirt to get cool. I feel so stupid asking for Gretchen's help. I didn't need help to walk into Ramona's apartment and kick at the garbage. I'm embarrassed and want to take it back when a knock on the door behind me makes me jump. Gretchen is on the porch, and I open the door, relieved to tell her I'm calling

the whole stupid thing off. "Mom can be here in about an hour."

"But I was going to—"

"Do you want me to follow you there, or do you want to ride together?"

I never thought things would move this fast, and my heart beats double-time. "I need to go somewhere afterward," I say, making it up as I talk. "So it'd be best if you followed me." She looks as relieved as I feel.

"I'll knock when Mom gets here."

I close the door and wonder what I need at Ramona's? What would I find and what would I put it in? A garbage bag? A box? Just an envelope? In the end, I leave the house with a box of garbage bags because I know where most of her stuff will go. Gretchen follows me the three miles to Ramona's, and my brain hurts trying to figure out what to say to her when we arrive.

The apartment house is a three-story, ugly light-brick building with shabby trees and cracked sidewalks. I can tell that Gretchen is sizing it up when she gets out of her car. This pit is as unkempt as Ramona always was. She follows me to the office door, and I realize for the first time that finding someone

here on Sunday will be next to impossible. I ring the buzzer and hold my breath, feeling uncomfortable with this stranger who's about to schlep through Ramona's junk. "Maybe no one's here on Sunday," Gretchen says. I ring the buzzer again and wait, staring at the cheap wood grain on the door.

A man with a balding head and potbelly walks down the stairs and faces us, smoke from his cigarette filling the small vestibule. He looks at me while squinting in the smoke. "You looking for me?"

"My mother was Ramona" is all I say.

He turns to go back up the stairs. "I wondered if you'd come."

We follow him, and our shoes squeak on the shoddy linoleum steps. If it wasn't for tacky Christmas wreaths hung on two apartment doors, you'd have no idea Christmas was just weeks away by visiting this place. The bald man sticks his key in the door and pushes it open, leaving us without another word. I run my hand along the inside wall, looking for the light switch, and a bulb flickers on the ceiling of the entry. The light illuminates the filthy floor, and I smell the pent-up dirt and dust inside the apartment. "I'll go find other lights," I say, leading Gretchen inside. My shoes stick to the linoleum as I walk to

the window and pull open the curtains. I turn to
look at the place and feel something heavy on my
chest, making my breath short. Papers, cans, liquor
bottles, rotten food, fast-food wrappers, and cereal
boxes—garbage is everywhere. I hold my hand
under my nose. "I'm sorry I asked you to do this."

Gretchen's already rummaging through cabinets
in the kitchen. "We just need some trash bags," she
says.

"I brought some," I say, walking to the door. "I
forgot them in the car."

"I'll get them," she says, holding her hand out for
my keys. I reach into my coat pocket and pull them
out.

Her eyes are big and soft. "This won't take long."

I hear her running down the stairs, and I feel
nauseated. I crack open a window and a blast of cold
air hits me in the face. I stick my head into the small
bedroom and look at the mattress and box springs
on the floor and wonder if that's where Ramona died
or if it was over there on the sofa or just in front of
the sofa on the filthy throw rug? I step through the
garbage in the bedroom and peer into the closet—
nothing in here but more garbage and a few pants
and shirts on the floor. I imagine some people go

through their parents' things with a swelling sense of grief from love and pride and gratefulness, but then there are people like me, who move things aside with their toe. This gulf of loss is different from grief. It's mostly dread and disappointment and regret.

"I'll take the kitchen," Gretchen says, startling me. She hands the box of garbage bags to me. "Should I ask you about what to save or—"

"If there's anything that can be used again, I'll take it to the secondhand store. From what I see, there's nothing here that I'll want." She nods and makes her way to the kitchen while I move to the living room.

The garbage feels sticky on my hand, and I use another garbage bag as a glove. I'm disgusted with every piece I throw away. "You lived like a pig, Ramona." I shove a hamburger wrapper and nearly empty bottle of booze into the bag along with a half-eaten can of Vienna sausages and a stack of magazines. "You never, ever, ever lived like a human being!" I sweep the garbage off the sofa into the bag and kick up the cushions, shaking my head. The couch is full of garbage and dried pieces of food. I throw the garbage away and stare at the stained sofa cushions that are destroyed. In an instant I

pick one up and heave it out the window. Out of the corner of my eye, I can see Gretchen, frozen at the kitchen sink, watching me. I lunge for the other two cushions and hurl them after the first. They lie on the asphalt below, looking small and ruined.

"Are you okay?"

Gretchen hasn't moved from the kitchen, but I can't turn to look at her. I nod and push more garbage into bags. On top of the TV is a picture in a black frame of Ramona and me standing in front of an enormous plastic cow. We saw it in front of a road-side restaurant as we were moving from one apart-ment to the next. "What a sight!" Ramona said. "Let's get our picture." The sun was bright, so I'm squinting up at the camera and Ramona is holding her ciga-rette aloft, looking as if she'd just taken me to Disney World. Propped up against that photo is a smaller shot of us taken in front of a stunted Christmas tree strung with popcorn next to an RCA television set on a metal stand. I glance around the room trying to spot any other photos or keepsakes, but there are none. The door closes and I turn behind me to see Gretchen putting two empty boxes on the counter.

"I ran down to the Dumpster to see if I could find a box for the plates and pots."

I didn't even know she had left. The dishes and pans clank as she fits them into the box, and she steps into the living room. "I threw away all the food. There wasn't much of anything but it was all open and stale or—"

"Ruined," I say.

"Everything she had is here in the boxes if you want to—"

I don't let her finish. "No. I don't want it."

We work in silence for the next hour or so. Gretchen hauls bags of trash down to the Dumpster, and a couple of times I hear her talking in the stairwell on her phone. Checking on her kids, I suppose. Three more trips are taken to the Dumpster, and on her return she walks beyond me to the bedroom and I hear her snap open a trash bag. I finish pawing through the garbage in the living room and then stand in the bedroom doorway. Gretchen has taken the sheets off the bed and is pushing the mattress off to see if there's anything under it. I help her lean it against the wall, and together we prop the box springs on it. The bed's metal railing looks like a picture frame around the trash that was under the bed. "Unbelievable," I say, snapping up a bag and pitching cans and bottles into it.

Gretchen works through a stack of magazines and papers on Ramona's nightstand as I reach for the garbage and clothes inside the closet. At one time, Ramona had nice skirts, dresses, and slacks that fell over her curves and long legs in soft lines. I pick up worn shirts, stretched-out sweaters, and holey pants and realize I can't give any of them to Goodwill.

"Melissa." I look up and see Gretchen standing by the nightstand holding a stack of papers in her hands. "This has your name on it."

She holds out a small envelope that has never been sealed, and I reach for it. I pull out a note-size piece of paper and read it. *Melissa, I know I haven't been much of a mother to you. You do have a brother and a sister you might like to . . .* I turn it over looking for more and laugh out loud. "You're kidding, right! This is it?" I keep laughing and lean against the wall, reading the note again. My eyes fill with hot liquid and I close them, pressing the note to my face. Thoughts and words buzz through my brain, but I can't pin them down. "All this time I was alone . . . with just her." I hold out the note and Gretchen walks over, taking it from me. "She never could give me anything that I needed. Not even now." A mixture of anger, resentment, and grief piles up

in my throat and I want to run. "No, 'Sorry, Melissa I really blew it.' Even now she won't take responsibility for anything. She couldn't even finish the letter!"

"But she started it." I look at Gretchen. Her face is solemn and plain but kind. "She could have started this months ago and just couldn't figure out what else to say and left it here at her bedside hoping for the right words."

I laugh up at the ceiling. "Ramona never lacked for words, believe me! Apparently, her problem was remembering she had more children! Messy lives don't usually create good recall." I shake my head. "She kept them from me. This could have brought some chance of happiness, you know, having a brother and sister? She couldn't stand the thought of any glimmer of a normal life for me." The silence in the room is too loud, and I take a step to get away.

"I'll help you find them."

I look at her. "I don't want to know them."

"Yes, you do." I open my mouth, but she talks over me. "You do. You would have wanted to know them when you were a child. If then . . . then why not now?" The thought terrifies and cripples me. What if they're like me? Or Ramona? "You said she

never gave you anything." She hands the note to me. "She did today."

It feels like my chest is in flames and I move past her, grabbing a bag of garbage from the bedroom and another from the living room on my way to the Dumpster. The air outside hits my lungs and I feel like screaming, crying, beating something. I don't know. The bags hit the side of the Dumpster with a thud, and I move to the couch cushions I had thrown out the window.

"How's it going?"

I look up to see the bald man; a cigarette is barely hanging on to his bottom lip. Smoke swirls into his eyes, making them slits in his face.

"Great," I say, heaving one of the cushions into the Dumpster. "Ramona's place is empty and ready for your next squatter. You or your tenants can take whatever furniture you want." I walk past him and open the door to my car.

"So that's that?" he yells after me.

"That's that," I say, sliding behind the wheel and closing the door. Sixty years of life. Done. Just like that.

Six

*It is our relation to circumstances that determine
their influence over us. The same wind that blows
one ship into port may blow another offshore.*
—CHRISTIAN NEVELL BOVEE

GRETCHEN

I take the kids to the new school and walk each of
them to their classrooms, then cry all the way back
to my car. Their little faces were wide-eyed and brave
even as they squeezed my hands right up to the last
second before letting go. New things are always so
hard.

It takes a while, but I find the cemetery and pull
into the parking lot, looking around. Two other cars
are here and I get out, shoving my hands into my
coat pockets. I haven't heard from Melissa since she

ran from her mother's apartment. There was a part of me that felt so sorry for her as we worked together in that atrocious space. I could hear her mumbling and cursing and see her throwing things out of anger and rejection, and my chest felt so heavy thinking about her growing up with the woman who had lived there. Then there is another part of me who can barely stand to be with her. It's too much like work. So why in the world am I here? I see two people in the distance near the back of the cemetery grounds and walk on a path through the headstones toward them.

Melissa's back is to me, and I watch as the wind picks up her hair and she shifts her weight from one foot to the other. Wisps of snow seem to fall from the trees and swirl on top of the ground. The undertaker nods and I step next to Melissa; her eyes are dark and tired looking at me.

"How'd you know?" she asks.

"Ramona's landlord knew she was being buried today. He told me before I left the apartment."

Clear liquid leaks from her nose and Melissa swipes at it with her hand. "Big turnout, huh?"

I look inside the hole at the simple box and won-

der if the state paid for this plot or how Ramona ended up here.

"Why are you here?" Melissa asks.

I pull my scarf tighter around my neck. "I've been to a lot of these. Men in my husband's unit."

"Heroes," she says, wiping the snot away from her nose again. "This is Ramona."

I look into the hole. "She was your mom, and everybody should have someone at their side when they bury their mom."

I sit behind the wheel of my car and watch as Melissa pulls away from the cemetery. The cold, the open grave, the memories of Kyle and his unit rattle my brain, and sobs from somewhere in my chest overtake me. I cry until my head hurts, my eyes are puffy, and my tissue is in soggy shreds.

I wipe my face with a napkin from the glove compartment before I step inside Mom's house. She's going crazy because she can't figure out how to fix this new life of ours, and if she sees that I've been crying, she'll worry the rest of the day.

Gloria is making her morning visit, and I smell

freshly baked something or other. "Cinnamon rolls," she says, putting one oozing with icing on a plate for me. I stare at it and Mom laughs.

"You must eat that because if you don't she'll leave it here for me and my trousers simply cannot take the pressure."

I take a bite and Gloria leans in, waiting for my response. I moan and she bangs the table with her hand. "See that, Miriam! We are going to *bake* a difference this Christmas!"

Mom rolls her eyes and I take another bite. "What's that mean?" I ask.

"Another one of her ideas," Mom says, filling a cup with coffee for me.

Gloria waves her hand in Mom's face to hush her. "Every year the chamber orchestra does a Christmas concert. This year all the funds from the admission tickets are going to Glory's Place to help the families we work with. And while that's a wonderful thing, the ticket price is only five dollars. It has always been five dollars and will always be five dollars, and that doesn't add up to much money at the end of the night. Well, I thought we could raise even more money by offering quality baked goods. You know, some people

don't have time to bake a pie or a cake for Christmas get-togethers."

"And others can't . . . or don't want to," Mom adds, winking at me.

Gloria waves at her to shush again. "So this year I think we can bake a difference by gathering really nice baked goods and selling them at the concert." She bangs the table again and Mom jumps, grabbing her head. "No brownies are allowed! Everybody always makes brownies. Cakes, pies, candies, and Christmas cookies only. No chocolate chips!" She spins in her seat and looks around. "For heaven's sake, Miriam! Where do you keep your paper? I have to write all this down."

Mom jumps up and glides in her pink satin robe to the drawer under the coffeepot, and I smile watching her. She's owned a pink satin gown and robe set for as long as I can remember. "Cakes, pies, candies, and cookies," she says, handing a notepad and pen to Gloria. "What's so hard to remember?"

"Let's think of good bakers in town." She puts the pen to her mouth and begins to think aloud.

"Oh, Gloria, please! Can't your brainstorming wait? Gretchen just got here."

"Don't stop," I say. "I love the idea. Put me down for something. Mom and I can surely bake a difference together." Mom refills my coffee and groans at the idea, sitting down with a swish and a swirl.

"You could ask your neighbor if she'd like to help," Gloria says, tapping the notepad. "What's her name?"

"Melissa. But I don't think she's the baking a difference type." Although Mom heard all about the apartment cleaning trip, I give Gloria the 411 of what happened, ending with the note.

"It is just so sad to me," Mom says. "I can't imagine not being a part of my children's lives to the point that neither of them would even know that I was dead."

"Now don't get worked up," Gloria says. "I'll make sure that your kids know that you're dead."

I smile and pat Mom's hand. "You were a great mother, Mom. Don't worry. You weren't anything like Melissa's mom."

"I never made you things like chicken and dumplings or cinnamon rolls."

"No. But you made lots of mac and cheese."

She makes tiny circles with her finger in the air. "Big deal."

"You showed up at every choir concert and musical."

Mom shoves a bite into her mouth and leans her head down on her hand. "Oh, yes! Those concerts could be brutal."

Gloria holds her cup with both hands. "What's Melissa like?"

"I don't know," I say, pushing my plate away. "She's just so odd to pin down."

"I'd be a bit wacky too, if I had a mother like hers," Mom says. She points her finger at Gloria. "Don't say a word, big mouth!"

Gloria laughs out loud and writes something on the notepad. "Just for that, I'm putting you down for two cakes." She looks at me and cocks her head; salt-and-pepper ringlets bounce on her forehead. "Why'd you offer to help her find her siblings?"

I sigh. "Because she's so pitiful . . . and if I had siblings that I didn't know about, I'd want to find them."

"But it seems you have so much on your plate right now," Mom says.

"I'm alone right now, Mom. I'm going to go home and clunk around in that empty condo. Trust me,

this will be a good distraction." She wants to say more but practices unbelievable restraint.

"She should call Robert Layton," Gloria says. "He's a lawyer in town and a longtime friend of mine. Miriam would latch onto him if he wasn't ten years younger than her."

Mom's cup hits the table with a thud. "Robert Layton is a married man, and if truth be known, he is a good five years *older* than I am." Gloria pretends to choke and Mom looks at me. "Do not encourage her, Gretchen. She is a child stuffed inside an old woman's body."

Gloria laughs out loud and takes another nibble of cinnamon roll. "Robert would know where to start in tracking down her siblings." She offers me another cinnamon roll. "Eat up, kiddo. These are so good you'll want to smack your mama. Which I'd love to see, by the way."

"You simply must eat another roll," Mom says. "Because if you don't Gloria will leave all of them here for me. This is what she does. She brings me fattening food and then gloats when I can't fit into my trousers."

Gloria smacks the table. "Ask Melissa to *bake a difference*."

"No, Glor—" I begin.

She holds up her hand. "Just ask her if she'll bake something to help raise money for people who can't pay their electric bill or buy their little boy a puzzle at Christmas. People want to help other people. They really do. Ask her. You never know what she'll say." I try to say something but she holds up her hand. "Ask her!"

I look at Mom. "She'll never shut up until you say you'll ask her. Trust me. She'll never, ever, ever, ever shut up."

I laugh and give them each a quick hug before I make my way to the door. "All right! I'll ask her to bake a difference. I'm off to surf the Internet classifieds for a job!" Mom's face gets long and somber, and I hurry putting on my boots. "Gloria? When do you need the baked goods?"

"On the twentieth, babe."

"The twentieth?" She nods and I slap my forehead. "That's the day my dad gets in."

Mom rises like a majestic pink cloud. "What?"

"Didn't I tell you?" I know I hadn't. "I invited Dad to come for Christmas."

"Here?"

I zip up my coat and look at her. "I want him

here, Mom. I want my dad and I want you." She is
slack-jawed and clutching the fabric of her robe on
her chest. "I haven't seen him since . . . I want him
here, Mom." She nods and I slip out the door with
what feels like a peach pit lodged in my throat. The
crappy thing about divorce is that you rarely get to
see *both* of your parents on holidays or birthdays or
any other day, for that matter. The fact is, my parents
are in their sixties and should be mature enough to
be in the same room without killing each other. I
don't think that's too much to ask at Christmas.

On my way home I drive around the square and
notice someone at Wilson's Department Store putting up a sale sign in the front window. Gifts have
been the furthest thing from my mind, and I pull into
an empty spot. Gloria's husband, Marshall, has
owned Wilson's for most of his adult life, and I keep
my eye out for him as I enter the door. The store is
lovely, with huge silvery snowflakes hanging from
the ceiling and a giant Christmas tree made from
enormous bulbs hovering over the jewelry counter.
Employees are dressed in gold, silver, or red blouses
and shirts and slacks. A sign for Santa's workshop
leads down the stairs, and Vic Damone singing "It's
a Marshmallow World" filters through the store.

After I browse the women's department for ideas for Mom I run downstairs to the children's department and Santa's workshop. As I reach the landing and make the turn for the final set of steps I run into someone carrying a large, plastic bin and packages tumble down the stairs. "I'm sorry," I say, reaching for two plain packages. "Melissa?" She picks up some envelopes at her feet and puts them into the bin. "Do you work here?"

"Did you think I was a doctor?"

There it is again. One of the reasons she's so hard to like. I ignore her question. "I was talking to a friend. Gloria. The woman who made the chicken and dumplings." I am amazed at how blank Melissa's eyes and face look when I talk to her. "She said her friend Robert Layton could begin tracking down your siblings." Something lights in her eyes.

"Are you kidding?"

It's not the response I was expecting. "No. She said he's a lawyer in town and could—"

"I work at his office in the afternoons."

I step aside so a customer can get down the stairs. "That's great! You could ask him if—"

She clutches the packages and heads downstairs. "I don't want to ask him."

I race after her. "Why not?"

She walks to a sales associate in toys and hands her a stack of mail. "I can't jeopardize my job there."

Melissa turns toward the shoe department, and I grab her arm. "Hold on. You'd pay him just like any other client." She starts to speak and I talk over her. "You want to do it." There's that blank look again. "You need to do it. The not knowing will drive you crazy."

Her face never changes expression. "I'll talk to Jodi about it."

She marches toward shoes again and I run in front of her. "One more thing. Do you bake?"

"Do I bake?"

"Gloria. My friend who—"

"Chicken and dumplings. I know."

"She has a place for families who need help. You know, like single moms and their kids, called Glory's Place. This year she's"—I make finger quotes in the air—"'baking a difference' to help raise money for them. You know, help them pay their electric bill or help with rent."

She shuffles the few pieces of mail in her hands. "I don't really bake, but . . ."

Kyle once said that the word *but* erases everything

before it, so I rush ahead before she says anything else. "You can come over to my place. Mom will come, too. We can all bake together." She nods with that same vacant face. "Just let me know."

I watch her walk away and look at my watch. I've been here five days. I have a feeling that despite what I think of her, one of these days I may actually see Melissa push herself up out of the rubble and crow.

Seven

Call it a clan, call it a network, call it a tribe, call it a family: Whatever you call it, whoever you are, you need one.

—JANE HOWARD

MELISSA

Gretchen nags me. Not in a physical way of always being around or in my face, but she's always in my head prodding and nudging me. I sort through the mail at Wilson's and hear her in my head telling me I want to find my siblings or I need someone to be with me as I bury Ramona. Maybe I don't want to find my siblings and could care less if anyone acknowledges Ramona's death. I rummage through the boxes and packages for each department and tell myself that I don't really want to know who my

siblings are, but it's a lie and I know it. Gretchen knows it.

Ramona has a half sister, Kay. I've only seen her on a few occasions, but one time, when I was a teenager and she and Ramona had drunk too much one night, she asked Ramona if some girl named Louanne was my sister.

"You know, Louanne? Jake's girl. I *know* you remember Jake," Kay said, laughing. Ramona shot her a look that could have ripped out Kay's spleen. "My God, you look just like each other," Kay said, looking at me.

"Shut up, Kay!" Ramona hissed. Kay withered a bit in her chair, and I was too frightened to ask any questions. All these years later I never asked Ramona a thing about that night, but it was the last time I saw Kay.

"Hi." I jump and turn to see a young kid standing in the mail room doorway. He has dark hair and a tall, lanky body. "I'm Josh. I was told to be here at eleven today."

I throw packages for the office into a bin. "For what?"

"Melissa's supposed to train me for the mail room."

I sort the letters in my arms and toss each one

into a slot on the wall. I look over my shoulder at a mail bin on the floor. "Well, I'm Melissa and that's the morning mail. We pick it up and put it into these slots. If it's a big package we put it into the bin with the department name." I kick at the bins on the floor with my foot. "If you have time you can deliver it right to the department. Otherwise, just leave it here and somebody will come get it. Everyday we receive some sort of merchandise and we help unload it into the stockroom or take it directly to the floor." I toss a few more packages into bins for security, ladies' wear, and jewelry. "There. You've been trained."

Josh walks to the mail bin and lifts out a few packages. "This just has a person's name at it," he says, reading the top envelope.

"A list of employees and which department they work for is right there," I say, looking at the wall to the left of the mailboxes.

He steps close to the list and glances for the name, putting the envelope into the slot for the children's department. "How long have you worked here?"

I'm not interested in chitchat with this kid and I sigh. "A while."

"Do you think it will be a problem if I have to take off suddenly someday?" Already he's scamming

for a way out of work. "My grandma is really sick, and my mom doesn't know if we'll just have to run out of town real quick."

I shrug. "Shouldn't be a problem. I'm sure there will be enough part-time help to cover you."

He reaches for more mail and is painstakingly slow finding the department name on each package. The buzzer rings in the mail room, and I sigh in relief. A shipment is at the loading dock, and that means I won't be alone with this kid anymore. "Come on. There's a truck that needs to be unloaded. Grab your coat."

Unloading the shipment and getting it on the floor or in the stockroom takes up the rest of my time before I leave for the law office. "Will you be working tomorrow?" Josh asks as I put on my coat.

"I'm here everyday with bells on," I say, leaving.

I usually walk through the city square to get to the office but today I'm especially hungry and realize I didn't stop for lunch and left it in the fridge at Wilson's. I walk the few extra blocks to get to Betty's Bakery, thinking of my aunt Kay and the girl she said could be my sister. The place is decorated with those big, papery snowflakes that hang from the ceiling, and a tinsel swag with ornaments hanging

from it is draped over the bakery case. I choose the empty booth in the corner and wait for a waitress. A couple of older women are sitting at the table next to my booth and chattering like magpies.

"I just want some soup and water," I say to the waitress when she hands me a menu.

"Vegetable beef or clam chowder?"

I hand the menu back to her. "I'll try the clam."

"Do the vegetable beef, babe," one of the older women says. "That clam chowder isn't fit for consumption."

The waitress turns to look at her. "Thanks for the rousing endorsement, Gloria. You're great for business."

"Sorry, Heather. I love Betty's stuff, but that chowder has got to go!"

"Vegetable beef," I say.

"Thatta girl," the older woman says.

I look at her, wondering, and then just come out with it. "Are you the Gloria who's friends with Gretchen?"

She smacks the table in front of her. "One and the same, and this old broad here is Gretchen's mother."

Her friend rolls her eyes and speaks through her teeth. "You have absolutely no tact when introduc-

ing people, Gloria!" She looks at me. "I'm Miriam, Gretchen's mother."

"I live next door to her. She gave me some chicken and dumplings you made," I say, looking at Gloria. "They were great."

Gloria jumps out of her seat and plops down on the bench across from me. "You're Melissa!" She reaches for my hand and puts her warm, soft palm on top of it, squeezing. "I am so sorry about your mother, babe." Something in her touch or in the way she said "babe" makes my throat quiver and I look down at the table, pulling my hand out from underneath hers. "Come on up here, Miriam, and let's eat with Melissa today." I don't have time to say no or tell them I'm in a rush. Miriam reaches for Gloria's coat and purse and hands them to her, taking her seat next to Gloria. "So, how are you, babe?"

It's the second time Gloria has called me babe, and I push a lump in my throat as far down as I can, trying to find my voice. "I'm fine."

She pats my hand again and smiles like she knows me. "Life is short. It's so, so short. Makes your head spin when you think about it." She squeezes her warm hand around mine and I don't pull away. "Were you close to your mother?"

I look at both their faces and wish to God that either one of them could have been my mother. I don't even know them but sense they are good and kind, decent, and soft. They were there when their kids wanted to play a game. They wiped runny noses and bundled up little bodies for playtime in the snow. They cooked meals and baked cookies, even if the meal was Hamburger Helper and refrigerated slice and bake cookies. "No," I say.

Gloria's eyes mist over, and I can't imagine why she's crying. "She never knew what she was missing. Isn't that right, Miriam?"

"Awfully tragic," Miriam says, nodding at me.

I bite the inside of my cheek and feel so stupid. Why am I so emotional? These women are strangers! Gloria pushes Miriam out of the booth and then slides in next to me, putting her hand on my arm and keeping her voice low. "It's harder to let go of a bad relationship than a good one. With a good one you've got sweet memories and kind words. With a bad one you just got a whole lot of unanswered questions and open wounds." I keep my eyes on the table. I can't speak and feel like a fool. "Don't ever think that tears are a bad thing," she says, somehow knowing that I feel like exploding. "Lord have

mercy! I've cried buckets in my lifetime. But Miriam here doesn't cry much." She leans in and whispers. "Afraid it will melt the wax." I laugh and Miriam hisses through her teeth. "I buried my first husband and cried myself sick. My son ran away from home and was gone seven years. I can't begin to tell you how many tears I cried over that loss. Grief takes a while, but joy does come." She wraps her arm around me and she's as warm and soft and sweet-smelling as I imagined. She squeezes my shoulder and then smacks the table, the silverware bouncing in front of me. "I know! Why don't you come on over for Christmas dinner? Miriam and I will be cooking for the whole gang, although Miriam doesn't really cook. But she has always wanted to pretend to cook sweet potato casserole, so that's what she'll be doing this year." I smile and Miriam shakes her head, unaffected.

I begin to say, "I don't really know anyone and—"

"Now don't make a lot of ballyhoo out of nothing," Gloria says, "because you know Gretchen and now you know us. And you can plainly see that we're about as simple as people come."

"I wish you would speak for yourself, Gloria," Miriam says.

I twist the napkin in my hand, glancing at Gloria. "Okay." I can't believe I've accepted an invitation to eat with strangers. "I'll be baking a difference, by the way."

She throws her arms in the air. "Gretchen asked you! Good girl!" She grabs her head as if a lightning bolt just struck her. "Did she tell you about Robert Layton?"

"I work for him, actually."

She bangs the table again, and Miriam grabs her head this time. "Would you please stop making that confounded noise, Gloria!"

"Well, this is just downright providential! Of all the people to work for in this town and you're working for somebody who can help you find your family."

Family. The word lodges in my throat and heat breaks out on my back. The search sounds so easy when Gloria talks about it, and she makes me smile. "It all still seems so crazy," I say. They're looking at me, waiting for more. "All these years I thought it was just Ramona and me. Now . . . someone else is out there who may not even want to know about me. It's a strange way to piece a family together."

"What?" Gloria says. "It means that your sib-

lings were adopted, and that's the most powerful, beautiful story of love there is, isn't that right, Miriam?" Miriam smiles. "Both of Miriam's children are adopted, and they are two of the most loved kids I've ever met. Love is learned, you know, and your two siblings were loved long before they were even born and have grown up in families of love. I just know it. And that means they will only have love for you, too."

I look at Miriam. "It's true," she says.

"For all I know, it's going to be hard to track them down," I say.

Gloria leans close to me. "Just keep a little faith, babe." I don't even react to that because I've never had any faith to begin with, let alone even a little of it. I wanted faith; the kind that Mrs. Schweiger had that just spilled over and out of her as natural as a breath, but I've never known what that's like. Gloria seems to read my mind and moves her hand to mine, patting it. "When you say 'I believe,' it has the same power as letting a tiger out of its cage."

Sometimes you meet people, total strangers, who feel like home. Even if that home is filled with noise and dysfunction and silence that is beyond bearing, it's still home, with its secondhand furniture, worn

comforters, and smiles from people who love you despite your lopsided personality and crooked moods. Gloria and Miriam make me feel like I'm home. "I'll talk to Jodi when I get to work in a few minutes."

Gloria lifts her fists into the air as if she just won a race. "How old are you?"

"Thirty-nine."

She nods, looking at me. "For thirty-nine years you never knew you had family out there. Now everything has changed just like that," she says, snapping her fingers.

The wind is sharp as I walk the few blocks to the law office, but I don't feel it against my face. My mind is crackling with what will happen in the days ahead. Somewhere there is a woman in this world who is my sister and a man who is my brother. I shake my head, still not believing that Ramona lived with that secret her entire life. My siblings could be wasting their days like Ramona did, living from bottle to bottle or they could be like Gretchen and Gloria and Miriam. I know how my luck runs, and I hold little hope that my siblings won't be like Ramona.

When I walk into the office I notice that Jodi isn't

in her office, and I wave at Susan at the front desk as I walk to the room at the back, where I work. I sit at the computer and type in the name Kay Hart. It's a long shot, but I'm hoping to find Ramona's sister still alive so she can tell me if I have a sister. A two-year-old obituary for a Gene Riggins in San Antonio pops up and I read through it, spotting Kay's name, "survived by his wife, Kay Hart Riggins." I have no idea if it's her. I never knew she was married, and Ramona never said anything. I do a search of the white pages in San Antonio for Gene Riggins and find a number. My cell phone is in my backpack, and I reach for it but realize that if Kay has caller ID she'll recognize my name. I decide to use the office phone and dial the number. It rings, but I can barely hear it over the sound my heart is making in my ears.

"Hello." Sweat sits on my lip. Is that Kay's voice? "Hello?"

I'm hoping that Ramona shared secrets with her sister and that Kay can tell me whether Louanne, whoever Louanne is, is my sister.

"Hello," she says again, sounding like Ramona.

I try to find my voice. Kay could be the key to letting the tiger out of its cage.

Eight

*Sometimes a neighbor whom we have disliked a
lifetime for his arrogance and conceit lets fall a
single commonplace remark that shows us another side, another man, really; a man uncertain,
and puzzled, and in the dark like ourselves.*

—WILLA CATHER

GRETCHEN

I like distractions. Some people can't handle them.
If something distracts them from their already
planned day, it drives them bonkers. Not me. I like
busyness because it keeps my mind from slipping
here or there. Gloria's Bake a Difference project
and helping Melissa find her siblings are great mind
occupiers for me. Since Mom and Melissa met on
Monday, I decided to strike while that iron was hot

and invited them to come over Friday afternoon to
start baking. Mom insisted we come to her house
since she has the bigger kitchen. I spent Tuesday and
Wednesday looking for a job and recipes online
and found great ones for turtle candies, German
chocolate cake, hummingbird cake, chocolate raspberry cake, and caramel candy. (I didn't find any
job postings.) I don't know which ones we'll end up
making, but all the recipes were supposed to freeze
well and Mom said we could store whatever we
made in her freezer until the bake sale.

I haven't seen Melissa this week. She's worked
late the last three days at the law office, but at eight
twenty, as I finish packing the kids' lunches for tomorrow, I notice her car pull into her driveway. I
creep down the hall to check on Ethan and Em and
see that they're asleep. This first week of school has
worn them out. I pull their door closed and walk to
the sofa, falling into it. This is always the worst part
of my day. Just sitting alone with everything quiet
except my thoughts that make a tremendous racket.
A knock startles me and I jump to my feet, peering
through the peephole in the door. Melissa is standing
on my dark stoop, and I flick on the outside light,
opening the door.

"Your mail was put in my box today," she says.

I take it and step aside. "Thanks. Come on in." I'm not sure if I'm inviting her because it's the neighborly thing to do or if I want to drown out the noise inside my head. She stands as if glued to the front stoop, and I motion with the mail. "Come in! Have you eaten?"

"I was going to have some cereal."

I lead her to the kitchen. "I have spaghetti." I open the fridge and take out the bowls of noodles and sauce I'd put in there a couple of hours ago. "It seems like I always have spaghetti because my kids love it." She looks uncomfortable just standing there, and I look at the table. "Have a seat. Would you like iced tea or water? Those are my only choices right now."

"Water's fine," she says, looking around. "Looks like you're all moved in."

I cover the plate of spaghetti and put it in the microwave. "For the most part. Still need to hang things, but my dad's coming to help with them." I reach for a glass and fill it with ice and water and set it in front of Melissa.

"Thanks." She moves the glass back and forth in

front of her, watching the ice. I don't know if something's on her mind or if she's tired or doesn't want to be here or a combination of all three. The microwave dings, and I set the spaghetti on the table. She stares down at it. "I haven't eaten spaghetti in years."

Her voice always sounds so tired or uninterested. "Years!" I say, getting a cup of hot tea ready.

"The fast-food restaurants I eat at don't serve it, and I never go out at night and I can't make it so, yeah, it's been years."

When the water's hot, I sit across from her and dunk the tea bag up and down in my cup. "You can make it. It's easy."

She takes a bite and I can tell she enjoys it. "No, I can't. I can't make anything, really. If it doesn't come in a box, I can't make it."

"Did your mom cook from a box?"

She makes a noise in the back of her throat. "Ramona cooked from a can and ate out of a box. Growing up, I thought my dad must have worked for either Campbell's or Kellogg's." She's quiet, but I can tell she's angry.

"You never knew him?"

Melissa laughs while taking another bite. "I

doubt Ramona knew him!" She moves the meatballs around on her plate and talks into one. "Your mom is great."

I reach for the Tupperware container of cookies behind me on the counter and open it, pulling one out for my tea. "My mom can't cook, either!"

"But she was there, wasn't she?" Melissa asks, wiping her mouth with a napkin. "She looked at your homework and sat across from you at the dinner table and showed up when you had a part in the sixth-grade play and searched the house for your stuffed bunny at bedtime. She did that, right?"

"Yeah, she did."

She's cutting a meatball into tiny pieces with her fork. "When I met her and Gloria, it was like being with a family I knew when I was a kid. That mom held on to my hand the same way that Gloria did. Like I meant something. That's the way your mom looked at me, and I knew that she and Gloria were great moms."

"Oh, Mom has her quirks, believe me," I say.

"And the only reason you know her quirks is because she was there," she says, sounding tired.

We use the silence to eat. My mother never could cook and she was terrible at crafts and spent way

too much time thinking about what to wear or how she looked, but she has been a great mom. I can't look at her and think any of the things that Melissa must think of her mother. I finish the cookie and look at her. "When I was a teenager my mom and dad divorced. We went from all of us under one roof to three of us and Dad across town in an apartment. He eventually met another woman and moved to Arizona and became part of her family. Her kids called him Dad because they were so young when he married Liz. I'd sit in tenth grade math class and think about those snotty-nosed kids calling my father Dad while I went home to a house without him in it." Melissa is quiet, awkward is more like it. It seems she doesn't know how to carry on a conversation so I carry on without her. "I blamed Mom for everything. She was married briefly before Dad, when she was young. I brought that up and told her she didn't know how to be married. It just seemed to me that she could have done more to keep Dad in our lives. I hated her, I think. I wouldn't talk to her for months. It was awful. I loved my dad. I loved them together. I thought they were good, that everything was fine. I didn't know what was wrong about them. I still don't know."

"Your mom never remarried?"

Finally, she speaks! I wasn't sure if she was even listening. I reach for another cookie. "She did. After divorcing Dad, she married a college professor named Len and he was a good man. They were great together, but . . ." I think about it. "But I missed her with Dad. I wanted my kids to know them as grandparents together, not apart. Dad's marriage failed several years ago but he still lives in Arizona. He has grandchildren there. His life is there and Mom's was with Len. Len was good to Mom and he was good for her. He kept her grounded. Maybe that was Dad's problem. Maybe he let Mom get the best of him. I don't know."

Melissa finishes and twists the napkin around her index finger. "What happened to Len?"

"He died a few years ago, and then Mom and Gloria became best friends. She's done more for Mom than anybody in this world," I say, laughing.

"Ramona never had anybody." She says it with such gavel-rap finality.

"No one?"

She untwists the napkin and starts wrapping it around another finger. "She had lots of men—good-looking men, some of them married, and she'd use

them for money and booze, something to eat, you know. They were after one thing but she didn't care. She played that game for a long time. Sometimes a guy would wise up and leave her alone but she could always find another idiot and string him along. Even when her looks started to fade she could still find some desperate fool. She never had one of them who stayed. Not one staying man or one staying friend."

"Do you hate her?" I'm surprised I asked that but watch her.

She drums her fingers on the table, the napkin looking like a poorly wrapped bandage around her middle finger. "I can't hate her. I hate everything she did and everything she didn't do. I hate everything she was, but I can't hate her. It doesn't make sense."

"Sure it does."

She slides her plate away from her and pushes her chair back. I can tell that Melissa thinks she's uncovered too much.

"Thanks for this."

I reach for the plate. "Hey!" I say, remembering. "Did you talk to your boss about finding your siblings?"

She looks small and sunken now. "He and Jodi weren't in on Friday when I wanted to talk to

them." She twists her mouth and rattles the bottom of the glass on the table. "And then I lost my nerve after that."

"Why?"

She looks exhausted and defeated. "I don't know. I've been trying to call my aunt and ask her about a girl she told me about years ago . . . a girl she said looked so much like me she could be my sister."

"Have you called her?"

"I did, but I hung up."

I'm not good at pep talks or encouraging people to buck up, but I give it my best shot. "So there's a chance your aunt knows something?" She nods. "Then that's a simple call. If the trail stops with your aunt, then what?"

Melissa looks at me with a look that says I know the answer as well as she does. "I look at Ramona's Social Security number every day," she says. "And I know she wrote that number down at each hospital she gave birth in. Those numbers are the key."

"So if it's that easy then . . . you know what? I'll do it." She looks at me. "Get the papers, fill them out, and I'll turn them in for you."

She looks shocked and confused. "No, no. I'll do it."

"When?"

"I don't know. I'll . . ."

"I'll do it tomorrow."

Her eyes begin to twinkle and her mouth turns up. "I will do it myself."

"No, you won't. Let me have the papers."

"I am not going to give you the papers. I will do it."

I cross my arms over my chest. "When?" She starts to open her mouth. "If I call the law office tomorrow and ask Robert Lawton if you turned the papers in, what will he say?"

"First of all, he won't take your call because you will have called him Robert Lawton and not Layton."

"He'll take my call. I can sound very convincing on the phone."

"Second of all, you don't even know Ramona's full name. Thirdly—"

"Three strikes. You're out! I'm calling and getting the papers tomorrow."

She stands and walks to the door. "No, you're not. I am getting the papers."

"So when I call and ask—"

She opens the door and walks to the stoop. "You are *not* calling."

"You just watch me, sister! I will call so fast it'll make your head spin."

I can tell she's laughing as she walks on the sidewalk to her condo. "You are a nosy neighbor," she says, her back to me.

"You're still baking a difference tomorrow, right?" I yell into the blackness.

"I don't bake!"

"Okay! Be at my mom's right after work. I left her address in an envelope in your mailbox."

Maybe it's because she's a good distraction or that my life doesn't seem so sad compared to hers or maybe it's because she's so different from me, but for whatever reason, I think I'm really starting to like that woman.

Nine

Friendship improves happiness, and abates mis-
ery, by doubling our joys, and dividing our grief.
—JOSEPH ADDISON

MELISSA

I sink into the sofa and stare at the phone. Before I
talk with Jodi at the office I really want to clear up
this Kay thing. If I don't get this over with, I really
believe that Gretchen will show up at the law office
and ask for the papers. I dig through my backpack
for the number and dial Kay's number again. The
phone clicks on the other end. "Hello."

I'm nervous and my breath is short. "Kay?"

"Yes."

"This is Melissa." She's quiet. "Ramona's daughter."

"Sure. Oh!" She's surprised and doesn't know what to say. That makes two of us.

"I saw on the Internet that your husband died two years ago. Sorry. I never knew you were married, but that's . . . sorry."

"We were married twenty-three years. I have two children. How are you, Melissa? Where do you live and—"

I don't let her finish. "I thought you should know that Ramona died a few days ago."

There's no noise on her end. "It's been a lot of years since I've seen her. I sent her Christmas cards, but a few years ago they started to come back to me and I knew she had moved again and didn't tell me. She always was such an odd—" She stops. "How'd she die?"

"Heart." She makes a sound in her throat. "Kay? Years ago . . . years ago you said I looked like a girl named Louanne. Do you remember that?"

"Louanne Delgado. Sure. You looked like sisters."

My heart speeds up when she says that. "Is she my sister?"

There's no sound. "What?"

"Is Louanne my sister? Is she Ramona's daughter?"

"Louanne is Jake and Adele's girl."

I'm not convinced. "Jake was one of Ramona's men, right?"

She laughs. "No! They worked together at the factory and Ramona tried every which way to get to him, but that man was married for keeps. Drove your mom nuts."

"How do you know nothing happened? Why do Louanne and I look so much alike?"

"I don't know! It's just one of them weird things when strangers look alike."

I'm getting angry, disappointed, or frustrated; I can't tell. "You know Ramona had two other kids, right?"

"No, I never knew that. How do you know?"

"She left a note, telling me. I thought maybe Louanne was my sister because you said something years ago and Ramona got angry."

"Bit my head off. I remember. She always was short-tempered. Wouldn't talk to me for a year or more after that."

"Maybe she thought you found her out. Louanne could be my sister."

"No." Her voice is soft. "It was a stupid thing of me to say. I was just teasing Ramona because I knew how much she wanted to get at Jake, and I

thought it was so strange that Louanne and you looked so much alike, but she's not your sister."

"She could be. She—"

Kay cuts me off. "Jake and Adele moved to Florida when Louanne was ten. He never even met Ramona until Louanne was twelve or so and he started working at the factory."

Air is squeezed out of my lungs and I hold the phone limp in my hand, hoping for something to say. In a desperate way, I was hoping Louanne would be the end of my search.

"I stay in touch with Jake and Adele," Kay says. "I've seen pictures of Louanne over the years and now you don't look anything alike. Isn't that funny?" I don't respond. "I'm sorry about your mom. There'll never be another Ramona."

"Let's hope," I say.

"Will you let me know if you find your siblings?"

I tell her I will and hang up, worn-out from it all.

Josh is clocking in at Wilson's as I'm getting off work. He's so different from the other teenagers Wilson's has hired every year around this time. He shows up several minutes before his scheduled time, and if he

owns a cell phone, I've never seen it. One teenage girl texted as she sorted the mail until Mr. Wilson saw her one afternoon. Her mail room career ended that day. She was crushed.

"Hi, Melissa," he says, hanging his coat.

"You're in time for the shipment," I say, grabbing the shipping manifest.

"My grandma's better, so I won't be bolting out of here one day after all." I'm ready to go but can tell he wants to tell me more so I wait. "She got out of the hospital, and my mom flew to New Mexico to bring her and Gramps to stay with us for a while."

I open the door so he doesn't draw this conversation out. "That's great. What was wrong with her?"

"She had a mild heart attack. She blames all the German food she's eaten all her life." He sees that I'm ready to go and reaches for the shipment manifest. "See you around."

There's something about the way his jaw clenches or his face turns solemn as he sets to work that is oddly familiar and I stop, looking at him. "Have a good one," I say, letting the door close behind me. Something has always bugged me about Josh, but I can't figure it out. In the end, he'll put in his four weeks of holiday work and will have been

just another kid who earned "i-something" money at Wilson's.

I take the stairs up to the break room to clock out and grab my coat and backpack out of my locker when a man stops me on the landing. "Excuse me," he says. "I'm trying to find something for my wife without her knowing it." He's holding a navy blue sweater in one hand and a yellow one in the other. "She's right over there with her mother." He lifts one of the sweaters toward two women in the jewelry department. "Which color do you think would be best on my wife?" All I can see is the profiles of the women, one is a brunette and the other has silvery white hair.

"I don't know," I say. "I'm not good at that sort of thing. You should ask one of the ladies on the floor."

He looks disappointed, but he shouldn't have asked a total stranger for shopping advice! "My son Josh works here. Do you know where I could find him? He'd have an opinion."

I glance at the two women and realize one of them must be Josh's grandmother that he told me about. "He's down these stairs," I say. "Just knock on the door." He heads toward the mail room, and for a second I watch Josh's mom and grandmother, trying to

see their faces. I catch a small glimpse of his mother's face and think Josh looks like her. Navy blue, I say to myself, stepping into the break room.

The skies are bright for my short walk to the law office. I'm skipping lunch today so I can get out early and head to Miriam's to help her and Gretchen bake. I don't know why, but I find myself looking forward to being with them and baking something, anything for the first time. Once when I was around ten or so I begged Ramona to buy some of those slice-and-bake cookies at the grocery store. She wouldn't do it, and I noticed two other shoppers nearby so I got louder. "Please, Ramona! We never have cookies. I'll bake them myself." The other women looked at Ramona and smiled in an isn't-she-cute way, and I saw they were on my side. "Please! Please! We never bake cookies. I'll clean up the mess, I promise."

"All right, lamby," Ramona said, smiling at the other women and tossing the roll of cookies into the cart.

When we walked to the parking lot Ramona set the bag of groceries in the trunk and pulled out the roll of cookies, bringing them into the car. I got excited when I saw her using her nail file to open the roll, thinking we'd get to enjoy some cookie dough

on the ride home. She managed to open the roll and scooped out a large handful. "Here," she said, hitting me in the mouth with it. "Open up." I started to push her hand away, but she yanked my hand down, pushing the dough into my face. "Eat it! You made a fool out of me over it so you open your big mouth again and eat this." I opened my mouth and Ramona shoved the dough inside. "Swallow it." I gagged trying to chew the sweet, gooey mound but Ramona shoved another handful into my mouth. The dough hung from my nose and off my chin and tears filled my eyes but I willed them not to fall. I vowed at that moment to never shed another tear because of her and dried up then and there like Arizona. One handful after another was pushed into my mouth and when the roll was nearly empty Ramona threw what was left out the window and started the car. My face and shirt were a sticky mess and I wanted to throw up but I acted like I wasn't sick. Ramona looked over at me. "Do you still want to go home and bake cookies with your mommy?"

Ramona was on the phone when I threw up the first time. I didn't make any noise; I didn't want her to know that I was sick. I kept a bag by my bed so I wouldn't have to go to the bathroom and I threw up

two more times. I threw the bag out the apartment window so she'd never have the satisfaction of knowing what she had done to me.

I bring the chill of outside with me as I open the door to Layton & Associates. Jodi is at her desk when I walk into the office, and I see she has the phone to her ear. I take my time hanging up my coat and scarf and untie and then retie my sneakers. When she hangs up, she waves at me behind the glass and I walk to her door, indicating I'd like to step inside. "Come on in," she says. I open the door as Jodi opens a file drawer at the side of her desk. Jodi is about my age, maybe older, for all I know. She runs several times a week, though, and is probably older than she looks. Her hair is light brown and hangs at her shoulders. She's married, but I don't know how many children she has, and I feel bad about not knowing. "How are you, Melissa?" This is as far as Jodi and I ever get, and I know she's curious why I'm standing in front of her.

"I was wondering if I could hire Mr. Layton's services?"

She shuts the file drawer and faces me. "Really?"

"I'd like to find a brother and sister I never knew about."

She smiles and walks around her desk. "Come on." I follow her to Robert's door, and she steps inside. Robert is typing on his computer and looks at us over his glasses.

"Hello, ladies." He stops typing and takes off his glasses. Jodi's smiling and my face is blank. I didn't think she'd tell him so quickly! I thought she'd get the ball rolling herself.

"Melissa would like to hire your services, Robert."

He leans back in his chair and crosses his arms, watching me. "What's happened, Melissa?"

I know I'm red in the face . . . from the wind, the cold, the heat in this office, or the fact that I've rarely spoken to this man who gave me my job. "I just discovered that I have a brother and sister that I never knew about." He waits for me to finish before he says anything. "I'd like to find them if you do that kind of work. If not, I'll—"

Robert smiles and puts up his hand. "You never knew about them?" I shake my head. "Isn't that something?" He smacks his hands together. "Let's find them!" He looks at Jodi. "Have her fill out Kate's papers."

I follow Jodi to her office and she opens a file

drawer, pulling out a file. "What are Kate's papers?" I ask.

She pulls a stack of papers from the file and raps them on her desk to straighten them. "Cases that Robert knows his wife would want him to work on." I don't know what she really means. "Pro bono." She hands the papers to me. "He'll do it for free."

"I didn't mean for him to—"

"I know that. Fill out the papers and let's get working on your case."

My case! It feels too sudden. "How long do these things usually take?"

She puts the file back into the drawer. "Depends. We found a biological mother about six months ago and it took one day. One day! Over a year ago we tracked down a father, and that took a few months. You never know." She opens another drawer and pulls papers out of a file and checks to make sure she's handing me the right ones. "These papers will help us get started. They ask for your biological parents' names, if you know them, along with their Socials, if you have that info. Some people don't even have a name. Just a hospital or a town. We'll take what you have and get started."

"Thanks, Jodi." I walk to the back room, where I close the door and slump to the floor, reading the papers. One line asks for my mother's name. Another line asks for her Social Security number. I stare at them for what seems like an eternity before I reach for my backpack. I had written Ramona's Social Security number down years ago and carried it in my wallet. I hold the tattered note in my hand and read the number over and over. I print RAMONA JUNE MCCREARY on one line and write down her Social Security number on the other. I run my finger over the words and numbers, and somehow I feel it. I've just opened the tiger's cage.

When I finish up at three thirty I walk to the front of the office where Susan is on the phone. I pull on my coat and hat and put the papers in Jodi's in-box. Susan taps on the box, gives me a thumbs-up, and then waggles her fingers 'bye in my direction. I take a breath and wave, opening the door.

I don't know if I'm excited or scared to death. I want to be excited, I say to myself. I want to pray like Mrs. Schweiger always did and have her kind of belief. I want to believe that my brother and sis-

ter would want to meet me and that they're good people. I want to meet them and tell them that they were the lucky ones; they got away. They never helped their boozy mother into bed or had cookie dough crammed down their mouths. They were the favored ones, the chosen ones. The blessed ones.

It's a little before four when I arrive at Miriam's house. Her home is decorated with simple Christmas lights draped over the shrubs and wrapped around the porch railing and posts. That must be Gloria's house next door with a Noel sign hanging on the door and evergreen and lights wrapped around the porch columns. I knock on Miriam's door and Gretchen's son opens it a crack, staring at me. What is his name? I can't remember.

"You're Melissa from next door," he says, opening the door wider.

"How are *you*?" I ask.

"My nana says you can't bake either, so this whole baking deal will be over with toot sweet."

"Now don't tell her such things," Miriam says, coming up behind him and putting her hand over his mouth.

He pulls her hand away and throws his arms in the air. "That is exactly what you said, Nana!"

"I know, but don't tell her such things."

He walks away, shaking his head. Gretchen steps into the entryway and holds her hands out at her side. "Well?"

"Well, what?" I ask, slipping off my shoes.

"Do I need to make a call?"

I hand my coat and backpack to Miriam and roll my eyes. "Your daughter can be very pushy."

"Don't I know it," Miriam says, whispering.

"I am not, Mother! Go put her coat away!" I follow Gretchen to the kitchen, where my nose goes into overdrive. Gretchen picks up a spoon and stirs something in a pot on the stove. "Well? How about it?"

"Leave her alone, Gretchen," Miriam says, motioning for me to sit at the table. "She'll tell us when she's ready." She sits across from me and slaps her hand on the table. "So, are you ready?"

I laugh and nod. "Yes. I turned them in today."

"Oh, that's splendid!" Miriam says.

"I don't know," I say. "I have this feeling in my gut that my siblings are going to be more like Ramona and not in the least like you two." It comes out faster than I realize and Gretchen smiles.

"Wow. That was pretty close to a compliment.

Give her something hard to drink, Mom, and let's see what else she gives up."

"I didn't mean it as a compliment," I say.

Gretchen bangs the lid of the pot down. "Too late. Caught you being nice." She washes her hands and looks at me over her shoulder. "All right. Up on your feet, you two. Let's get a move on. Wash up."

The front door bangs closed and Miriam jumps, clutching her chest. "Gloria!"

Gloria peeks her head into the kitchen. "Aha! I was at home but had this creepy feeling, as if something was wrong over here. Now I see. Miriam's in the kitchen!"

Gretchen laughs and pulls out two big mixing bowls from a cupboard. Gloria rears back and opens her arms. "How are you, babe?" She hugs me to her, and I find myself hugging back. "Has it been a hard week?" I feel everyone's eyes on me and don't answer. Gloria wraps an arm around my shoulder. "Good days are on the way. Starting today! What are we baking, Gretchen?"

"Hummingbird cake and a chocolate raspberry cake."

Gloria pounds the countertop and makes yummy

noises. She pushes up her sleeves and moves to the sink. "Tell me what you need, doll."

"Okay," Gretchen says. "You help Mom make the raspberry one, and Melissa and I will take care of the hummingbird."

Gloria shakes her head. "I knew you'd stick me with your mother."

Miriam laughs out loud, and I find myself smiling, listening to them. Gretchen puts me in charge of measuring out the flour, sugar, baking soda, and salt while she gets the pans ready. "I haven't helped bake a cake since I was a kid and helped Mrs. Schweiger from next door," I say, remembering Mrs. Schweiger and I crammed into her tiny apartment kitchen making a mess with flour and sugar.

"So you have baked something!" Gretchen says.

"Not really. Mrs. Schweiger did everything. I was just there to lick the beaters and eat the frosting."

When I'm done with the dry stuff Gretchen asks me to mash some bananas with a fork. I've eaten plenty of bananas but have never mashed one before. I press the fork into it and Gretchen laughs. "You don't have to be nice to it. Just mash it down." I mash away, and Gretchen opens a can of pineapple and chops up some nuts.

"These ingredients don't sound like they'll be good together."

"You'll be amazed," Gretchen says, chopping the pecans.

I am fascinated by the simplest act of pouring oil, breaking eggs, and using the mixer. I'd never had reason to use one before and find myself grinning.

"For crying out loud, Miriam," Gloria says on the other side of the counter. "Grate the chocolate, not my nerves."

Miriam sighs. "I am trying my best, Gloria!"

"Are you trying to lull that chocolate to sleep? Grab a hold of it like you mean business and start working it over the grater."

"I want to switch teams," Miriam says, holding the grater in the air.

I laugh and read aloud the instructions of how to blend the rest of the ingredients. The bowl is awkward in my hands as I pour the batter into a pan. A huge glob of batter slides down the outside of the bowl and Gretchen swipes at it with a spatula. I'm leaning over the next pan when Gretchen's cell phone rings. She excuses herself to the living room, and Gloria and Miriam exchange glances.

"He's not just standing today! He's walking!"

Gretchen says, running into the kitchen. The phone is still next to her ear. "They're sending him to Texas." She dashes back to the living room, and Gloria hugs Miriam, whose eyes are filling.

"Who's walking?" I ask, setting my sloppy bowl down.

"Kyle," Gloria says.

"Who's Kyle?"

"Her husband," Miriam says, laughing and crying at the same time.

"But I thought her . . ."

Gretchen hangs up the phone and flings herself into Miriam. Gloria wraps her arms around them, and they are a mass of arms, hair, and tears. Gretchen breaks away, laughing, dabbing at her eyes with her sleeve. She looks at me and I'm frozen in place. "I thought your husband was . . . you never told me he was alive," I say, feeling stupid as soon as the words slip past my teeth.

Gretchen reaches for a tissue. "You never asked."

"Was that Kyle or the doctor?" Miriam asks.

"Dr. Larimer," Gretchen says, her eyes pooling again. "He said Kyle tried to move his legs to the side of the bed again today and asked the nurse to help him stand. Dr. Larimer said it took all his

strength but he put his feet down and lifted off the bed. Kyle wouldn't sit back on the bed like they asked but stood there for ninety whole seconds before he took some steps!" She lifts her arms in the air and waves them around.

"I thought he—" I stop. I never asked. Gretchen's words keep firing into my ears and my head feels hot. I never asked Gretchen one thing about her husband. Ethan had said he had gotten hurt but I never asked what that meant; I assumed he was dead. Since I have met Gretchen I have done nothing but ramble on and on about Ramona; I've never asked about what I presumed was her dead husband or her marriage to him. I sat in her home and ate spaghetti and didn't ask the questions that I thought would make me uncomfortable. I didn't even ask about her children, who were sound asleep down the hall. She looks at me and I know this is my one shot at a friend, but even now I don't know what to say. "I thought he was . . ."

Gretchen hands a tissue to her mom. "It's okay. I thought he was, too, for a while there."

A flash of anger balls inside my chest. "No! I met you and Ethan and he told me about his dad and a bomb but I didn't say anything. I just stood there." I

step past them and head to the entryway, where my coat is hanging. I can't be here right now. This moment doesn't include me.

Gretchen follows. "Where are you going?"

I reach for my coat and put my arm in a sleeve. "You need to be with your family and friends right now."

She pulls the coat off my arm and holds it to her chest. "I am." Her face is soft, and Miriam and Gloria peek around the kitchen door, looking at me.

"I'm not a friend," I say, keeping my voice low.

"Then what are you?"

I feel like an idiot. "I should have asked."

Gretchen hands my coat to me and raises her eyebrows. "We're not finished baking, so come back in here and ask whatever you want."

I fumble with the coat in my hands. I've blown so many things in my life. I've never had this, whatever this new thing is that I have with these women, and I don't know how to act with them. Half the time I don't know what to say, but I do know I don't want to ruin it. I hang up my coat and walk back to the kitchen to finish our cake.

Ten

*Every morning I wake up saying, I'm still alive; a
miracle. And so I keep on pushing.*
— JACQUES COUSTEAU

GRETCHEN

The Eighty-second Airborne Division had been de-
ployed to the southern region of Afghanistan in Au-
gust of last year. Kyle's MOS (military occupational
specialty) was infantryman, and he had risen to the
rank of Sergeant First Class. His fifteen-month tour
(his second in Afghanistan) would be over in November, twenty years in the army would be complete, and
he'd be home for good. No more moving around.
No more shipping out.

On Kyle's first day in the province he found a
small circle of children to kick a ball with outside

the base. He and several men in his unit always found time for the kids in Afghanistan. He said they were always sweet and loving and ready to play. On that morning, September fifteenth, he had gone out to the kids and kicked the ball around with them. They had things like cans or empty food sacks that they used for bases, and on that morning Kyle noticed that one of the food sacks looked fuller, but he thought it was nothing more than the wind that puffed it out. The children threw the ball here and there, not really playing any sort of real game when Kyle suggested they kick it like they had in days past and run the bases. Some of the little ones wanted Kyle to kick it hard, as he had done the day before, and he kicked it so the kids would have to run for it and he took off running. Two other guys from the division were cheering on the kids to get the ball before Kyle made it home, and he pretended to be out of breath running the bases. He ran to first and a little guy around six tried to hold him there, and then Kyle took second with the little guy still hanging on to him. Kyle ran on with the little boy dangling from his waist, not knowing that third base was a bomb.

The report says it blew Kyle thirty feet. It took his arm, part of his head and left him unconscious.

Rocks and metal pierced his face, neck, jaw, and chest. The mother of the little boy who had been clinging to Kyle bent over the tiny broken body and clung to what was left of her son. A medic pinned a tag with the word *expected* on it to Kyle's chest, meaning he was expected to die as they transported him to the army hospital in Landstuhl, Germany.

The kids and I were going to move from our home in the little town of Spring Lake (near Fort Bragg) into our new house in Grandon that weekend, but then the phone rang. "Is this Mrs. Daniels?" I just knew the call was about Kyle, and I knew that something had gone horribly wrong. He told me who he was, but I couldn't tell you his name today if I tried. "A bomb exploded, and your husband . . ." I don't remember my knees buckling but recall the feel of the floor on my forehead as I pressed the phone to my ear to drown out *Go, Diego, Go!* on TV. My arms shook as I picked up the remote to turn it off. I hung up the phone and called upstairs to Emma, but my voice was gone.

When Kyle shipped off to Afghanistan the first time, he said, "It's nothing like it was when my grandfather fought," he said, referring to World War II. "They stormed the beaches, and thousands of men

died a day." I wasn't sure how that was supposed to reassure me. He hugged me close. "It's not like that anymore, Gretch. We haven't lost as many during this entire conflict as we lost on one day at Iwo Jima." But the thought of receiving a phone call was always there in the back of my brain, and now it was real.

Ethan whined, begging me to let him finish *Go, Diego, Go!* I knelt down and clutched him to me, burying my face in his neck. Emma knew something had happened to her dad when she stood on the landing at the top of the stairs. She saw me clinging to Ethan and wouldn't come down, waiting for me to say something.

"Dad's been hurt," I said. She burst into tears and ran down the stairs, falling into Ethan and me.

Mom flew to North Carolina and stayed with the kids, and I flew to Germany. That was the longest flight of my life. I didn't eat; I didn't sleep; I couldn't read. I just prayed. I wasn't angry; I was frozen by the thought of what we are capable of doing to each other. Someone, an unknown face and name, left a bomb where children play in the hopes of killing one of us. It didn't matter that a child or several children could die as well. They were collateral damage and nothing more. Tears fell to my

hands when I thought of the mother who still had to live there, passing her son's killer in the street or haggling with him over the price of fruit in the marketplace. There would never be any answers for her, just an empty place at her table. Kyle was alive, if even barely, he was alive. He didn't come home with a military escort. The mother wasn't even afforded the dignity of an escort for her son.

When I landed I learned that a small piece of metal had been lodged near Kyle's jugular vein and that he had nearly died during the surgery. My heart pounded in my head as the doctor explained all that *almost* went wrong with the brain surgery and all that could still go wrong. They had placed him in a medically induced coma, and they would keep him in a coma to give his brain time to heal and rest. "For how long?" I asked.

"It varies," the doctor told me. "But with his injuries I think it can be expected that his brain will need at least a month." I couldn't breathe or feel my legs. How could I explain this to the kids? The doctor tried to prep me for how Kyle looked, and even though I said I was ready, I wasn't. His right arm was missing below the elbow and his head was swollen twice its size on one side with a hollowed-out

part on top. Dark red scars with black thread were laid out like tracks over his head, neck, face, and chest and his face looked battered, but it was his eyes that were so unnerving. They were half opened when I walked into the room. They made me jump because I expected them to be closed, but they'd follow me around the room. I kept talking to him, expecting him to pick up a finger or wiggle his foot or something, but nothing happened. He just kept following me with his eyes. I could see him, I could touch him, but it didn't feel like it was Kyle in the bed.

"Does he know it's me?"

"Maybe," the doctor said. He said it in such a way that made me feel he was saying that for my benefit but that Kyle was still somewhere far off inside his brain.

I sat on the bed next to him and held his face, staring into those half-opened eyes. "Come out, Kyle. Come out of there," I begged. "Oh, God! Tell Kyle to come out. Please." I kissed his head. "Please."

Tom and Alice, Kyle's mom and dad, arrived the next day, and I couldn't imagine what they were seeing. What if that was Ethan in that bed? My mind couldn't comprehend what they were feeling. For

the next few weeks I held Kyle's hand and held up
pictures of the kids for him to see through those
half-opened eyes. I told him I loved him and would
take his broken, shelled body home with me as soon
as I could. Doctors had no idea the extent of Kyle's
brain damage but always prepped me for the worst:
he may never talk like he once did; he may not be
able to walk without assistance; he may never drive
or be able to brush his teeth. They showed me the
X-rays of his brain, and it looked like someone had
scooped out a part of it and tiny pieces of rock
floated in midair around his head and face. I put my
lips up to his head and prayed as I've never prayed
before. I prayed for a miracle, a sign, a new brain for
Kyle. The week I arrived I didn't eat for five straight
days. I never left his side.

On day thirty-two, doctors began pulling him out
of the coma. In the wee hours of the thirty-fourth
day his hand began to quiver. My heart drummed
in my ears and I jumped out of my chair and leaned
closer to him, squeezing his hand. He squeezed back
and I touched his face. "Kyle, it's me. Can you open
your eyes? Can you see me?" His lids must have
weighed fifty pounds; it took him so long to lift
them. When he did, he tried to grin.

I crawled into bed with him and yelled for the doctor. Kyle was shocked to see them. He thought we were alone somewhere but didn't have a clue where that was! He tried to speak, but the words were garbled and I could see in his eyes that that confused him. Doctors tried to explain what had happened to him, and when they did, his eyes glistened. "None of the other men were hurt, Kyle," I said. "Just minor wounds. That's all." It would be more than a week before I told him about the little boy.

"He's trying to talk," the doctor said, smiling at me. "That's a good sign."

When we were alone I leaned close to Kyle and kissed him. "I know you're going to fight this out, Kyle! I know you're going to push yourself up out of the rubble and crow." His eyes were still, but I could see him in there. "Remember? Remember the rooster? That's you! You are getting out of this bed, and you are going to talk and walk and drive a car. Do you hear me?" He babbled something unintelligible, and I wiped my eyes. "Oh, yeah? Well, you've never listened to me before. Why start now?" His mouth tried to turn up, and I kissed the caved-in part of his head. "Remember the green SUV? I told you not to buy that truck and what happened?" His eyes were

dull, looking at me. "It left us stranded on the high-way . . . twice! That orange shirt? I told you orange was a horrible color on you and what happened? People always mistook you for a traffic cone." He attempted a grin again, and I squeezed his hand. "But this time you're going to listen to me. I'm giving you eight weeks to get home, Sergeant Daniels!" He closed his eyes, and I knew he was in there somewhere with fragmented pieces of the kids and me and of an orange shirt that could stop traffic.

"Max!" I jumped in my chair beside Kyle's bed and looked at him. It was the middle of the night and his eyes were closed. "Max! Maxey!" Max was our first dog, a big, lovable Lab mix. It was two days after he came out of the coma and the first words he spoke plain as day. I laughed out loud and told him we'd have a chat later about him saying a dog's name before mine.

I never went back to sleep but watched him throughout the morning, praying he'd wake up talking and wanting to take charge. I was staring at him when his eyes opened. "Bug," he said.

I bent over laughing. First a dog and now a bug!

The word sounded thick, medicated and slurred, but I understood him.

"Apple," he said.

I couldn't stop laughing as I called the doctor.

"General."

Kyle always called me "General" when he was at home, indicating that I outranked him. "Now you're talking," I said, lying down next to him and kissing his face.

When he was able to string together clumps of three or more words over the next several days, Kyle began to ask about our life together. It took him ten minutes to remember Emma's name and he never remembered Ethan's; actually, he didn't remember Ethan at all. He could say Emma, but Ethan caused him trouble; he couldn't say the *th* without struggling. I spent much of the day pointing to things and saying the names of them so he could repeat after me: cup, water, ice, lamp, blanket, pillow, socks, underwear, nose, arm, hair, coffee, eggs. We went over the same words again and again because so many of them weren't understandable. He scrambled the letters the first few times he said the alphabet, but after several tries he made it from *A* to *Z* in less than ten minutes.

Each day a physical therapist worked his limbs to help him regain strength, and Kyle grew more determined to get out of bed on his own. On Thanksgiving Day, I sat on the bed beside him and we called Mom to check on the kids. It was more than two months after the bomb exploded and the first time Kyle attempted to talk to the kids, and in his head he thought he was talking fine but they struggled to understand him. He was quiet when we said our final good-byes to the kids, and I knew what he was thinking. "It's hard to understand over the phone," I said.

He was still the rest of the day, and I knew the phone call had taken a lot out of him. The next day he woke up, looked at me, and said, "You need to go home."

I put my hand on the little sprouts of hair on top of his head. "What?"

His eyes were liquid blue. "The longer you're here—" He stopped, reaching inside his brain for the next words. "They'll think I'm dying." I knew he meant the kids, and I started to say that Mom would assure them that he was getting stronger every day but he stopped me. "My mom and dad are here. Go move. Get them in school."

I swung my legs off the side of the bed, looking at him. "No, Kyle!"

"They'll be rushing—" He stopped, thinking. "Working—" He looked at me. "When you do a lot?"

"Busy?"

"They'll be busy and won't think I'm dead. Now they're home thinking the worst."

In a way, I knew he was right. The kids and I were always nervous when he returned home after being away for months at a time. We got into a rhythm of how things worked without Kyle and worried that he'd feel left out or that we didn't need him on a daily basis. I couldn't imagine how Emma and Ethan felt about his coming home now with so many injuries. They weren't even sure what those injuries were or what Kyle could or couldn't do. I dreaded leaving Kyle, but he was right. After the kids heard his voice they needed to know that he was okay.

He moved his hand to my leg and squeezed. "They need you. Go move and then—"

I put up my hand to stop him. "Hey! I'm the General, remember? I'll get us moved, but then I'm coming back."

He smiled. "I'll be walking for you."

"You mean you'll be walking *to* me!"

I had been e-mailing pictures of Kyle all along, but before I left, his mom took several of Kyle and me together to show the children that we were still a team and he was doing okay. Although I didn't really know what okay would look like for us now, I could tell Em and Ethan that he was alive and getting stronger every day. What more can any of us ask?

Eleven

In faith there is enough light for those who want to believe and enough shadows to blind those who don't.

—BLAISE PASCAL

MELISSA

The ringing makes me jump and I stumble out of bed, racing to the kitchen. "Hello," I say into the receiver.

"Melissa, it's Pat." My supervisor at Wilson's. I squint to see the clock on the microwave. It's five in the morning. "Josh has been in an accident." My brain struggles to remember who Josh is. "He was on his way to work." Josh in the mail room! "Can you come in this morning?"

I haven't worked on a Saturday in ages and try to recall what I have to do today but come up blank.

"Sure. Yeah. I'll shower and be right in." Images of Kyle fill my mind. "Wait! How bad was he hurt?"

"All I know is he's at University Park Hospital."

At least four inches of new snow lie on the ground, and my tires slide when I back out of the garage. The roads are icy as I make my way slow and sure through the town square. For the first time in my life I can say I love it here. I love the sleepy streets and the three fir trees that are decorated for Christmas next to the gazebo. I love the dorky plastic Santa in the drugstore window and the evergreen wreaths that hang on each window of the fire station. Ramona died and I finally feel at home. I hope someday someone can explain that to me. Snow falls as if it's sluggish, taking its time, and I think of Kyle, his legs no stronger than these puffs of snow and I realize I've never known anyone who has served in the military, let alone someone who has fought in a war. I'm embarrassed because I've never thought about what they do or the families they leave behind, who try to maintain some sort of normal without them.

I enter Wilson's through the loading dock doors and make my way to the mail room. The shipping manifest shows a shipment is due at six this morning. I prep the shelves in the stockroom, although I know

the shipment will be late due to the roads. When I finish, I walk to the office to see if by chance anyone is in yet. The office is dark and I check the door. It's open. I walk inside and flip on the lights, looking around. I know if I call the hospital that they'll never give me any information about Josh. Several file cabinets sit behind Judy's desk, and I wonder if one of them contains phone numbers for Josh or if his information would be on the computer.

I move to one of the file cabinets and try my luck there. I pull open a drawer, and it contains names of others businesses—vendors, I assume. I pull open each drawer and scan the files, looking for names I recognize. The third file drawer contains some names I recognize as employees, and I search for Josh, realizing I don't know his last name. A file for Joshua Dumont catches my eye and I pull it out, reaching for a sticky note and a pen off Judy's desk. I scan the file for phone numbers and write down his cell. For some reason, I take down the number for one of his emergency contacts, his parents, Mike and Karla Dumont, and jot down his home address. I slip the file back into the drawer and turn the lights off as I leave the office. Somewhere, the night security guard is either watching the cameras or

walking through the store, so I act as if I was supposed to be in the office at this hour in the morning.

It's six fifteen when I make it back to the mail
room, and I take my cell phone out of my coat pocket.
I set the sticky note on the countertop and call Josh's
cell. I don't know if I'm thinking he'll answer or
someone else will pick up his phone, but for some
reason I need to know what happened to him. His
phone rings one time and goes directly to voice mail.
I hang up and look at the other number on the paper.
I can't call his parents. I'm not his supervisor calling
to check on him. I'm not anybody.

It's one o'clock when the shipment is unpacked
and the mail is distributed, and I clock out for the day.
I'm heading toward home when I find myself sitting
in the parking lot of University Park Hospital. I
kept telling myself that I wouldn't come, that I'd
drive straight home and watch something on TV,
but I wandered onto the highway and ended up
here. I've never visited anyone in a hospital before
and am not sure how to find Josh. Two women sit
behind a huge C-shaped desk in the entryway, and
I walk toward them, hesitating, ready to go back to
the car because I'm not sure what to say to Josh. "Can
I help you?" the younger of the two women asks.

"I'm here to visit Josh Dumont. He was in a car accident this morning."

"Are you a family member?"

My palms feel sweaty, and in a stupid way I feel as if I've done something wrong. "No. I'm a fr—I work with him."

She holds a pencil with both hands and lifts it right in front of her face. "We can't give out that information. A family member would have to let you know if he's here."

I turn to leave, feeling embarrassed and ridiculous. Deep down, I knew it was a dumb idea to come.

"Do you know Josh?"

A middle-aged man holding a small white sack is standing beside the desk. He looks familiar, and then it hits me. I blew him off when he asked which sweater would look better on his wife. "I work with him at Wilson's," I say, hoping he won't remember me.

"I'm Mike. Josh's dad."

He doesn't remember me. I don't shake his hand or hug him or do anything but stand here. "Our supervisor said Josh was in an accident this morning and I wanted to . . ."

"Come on up," he says, walking toward the row of elevators. "He had surgery first thing, but he's out

of recovery and in his room now." The elevator doors close and Mike pushes the number eight.

"What happened?"

"Icy roads. A van lost control, slamming into Josh on the passenger side. He stepped on the brake when he saw the van sliding toward him and because his leg was braced for impact"—he straightens his leg to demonstrate—"when the van hit him, the force broke the low part of his tibia. They got him right into surgery, and it took a couple of hours. They put a pin in. They're keeping him for two or three days."

The doors open and I follow Mike down a bright hallway. "He probably doesn't want any visitors," I say, dragging behind him.

He stops and looks at me. "Who wouldn't want to see a friend after coming out of surgery? He'll love it. My wife went home to pick up Lyda, Josh's grandmother."

Josh's leg is raised in some sort of sling, and he's propped up on pillows when his dad and I walk into the room. "Melissa!"

I stand at the foot of the bed and lift my hand to wave. "I heard what happened and just wanted to see that you're . . . come say hi." Mike hands Josh

the sack, and Josh pulls out some fries. A tray with traces of something brown and bland sits at his bedside.

"They made me eat that," Josh says, grinning. "But I had to have some fries to chase it down."

"I'm sorry about your leg."

He takes a bite of a fry and smiles. "I'm hoping I'll have years of fun setting off airport security."

"How long do you have to be off it?"

His mouth is full and ketchup sits on his upper lip. "Six weeks."

"So I guess your days are done at Wilson's?" He shrugs, eating. I swing my arms, looking around. "I should have brought you something, like a magazine or a bag of chips or something." I shove my hands in my coat pockets to keep them from moving and realize I must look as awkward as I feel. "Well, I need to get going. I just wanted to check on you and make sure you're okay."

"Come back anytime," Josh says. "I like jalapeño kettle chips."

He grins while eating, and I wave good-bye to Mike. I wait for the elevator and stand aside when it opens. Four people step out and I watch as two of them, a middle-aged woman carrying a suitcase and

a white-haired elderly woman, make their way as quickly as they can down the hall. Josh's mom and grandma. I let the elevator doors close without getting on and strain to hear them in Josh's room. I can't make out any words but I hear laughing and the rise and fall of voices. My eyes fill and I press the button for the elevator.

I knock on Gretchen's door when I get home because, well, just because. I've been alone so much of my life that I'm sick of it. "Did you have to work today?" she asks, opening the door. It smells like something chocolaty in her house, and I hear the kids down the hall; it sounds like they're dismantling their room.

"I was called in this morning because a kid was in an accident."

She leads me to the kitchen. It's a mess of dirty bowls and lunch plates. "What happened? Was he hurt?"

"Broke his leg. I saw him in the hospital."

"Did he have to have surgery? Is he okay?" I sit down at the table and look at her. "Is he okay?" she asks again.

"How many times have you asked that in your life?"

She looks at me like I'm crazy. "What are you talking about?"

"Do you know how many times I've asked that?"

She leans against the counter and crosses her arms. "I don't know what you're talking about."

"I don't think I've ever asked if someone was okay."

"Sure you have."

"No! I haven't. I've never visited anyone in the hospital, shown up at anyone's funeral, baked a cake for a fund-raiser, or batted an eye when I heard someone in the military had died."

Gretchen turns on the light in the oven and mumbles as she peers inside at what I know is another cake for the Bake a Difference fund-raiser. She sits down across from me. "You just said you went to the hospital, so you *have* visited someone in the hospital."

"First time."

"And you *have* baked a cake for a fund-raiser."

"One time."

She gets up and crosses to a cabinet, pulling out two glasses. "There's a first time for everything." Her voice sounds strained as she puts ice in each glass and fills them with water.

I watch her and know that Gretchen is my friend. She is my friend for no particular reason other than she moved next door and cleaned out a crappy apartment and showed up at the graveside of a stranger, invited me in for spaghetti, and asked me to bake a cake. "Ramona never . . ."

She hands me the glass of water. "Ramona's dead." She is blunt and seems frustrated. "I don't know what you're going to say . . . that she didn't make you be a caring person because she was so self-absorbed or whatever. It doesn't matter. Whatever she did or didn't do . . . you can't change your past. Not even God can change your past."

She stops short of telling me to shut up and grow up. Two weeks ago I would have gotten up and walked out, but today I feel relieved. Gretchen is my friend for no particular reason at all and most particularly because she puts up with me.

I awaken at three, thinking of Josh. I roll over, rearranging the blankets, and see his mother and grandmother scurrying down the hall toward his room. "What's happening? Show me," I say aloud in what I realize is a prayer. It's three fifteen when I

look at the clock again and I roll over to my other side, the image of Josh's grandmother running through my mind. What did his dad say her name was? At three thirty I'm frustrated because I can't sleep. What was his mom's name? The grandma's name? At four thirty I sit bolt upright in bed. Mike said her name was Lyda!

My heart is racing as I lie back down. I smile in the night and feel like a kid again. I'll never get back to sleep now.

Twelve

Christmas waves a magic wand over this world,
and behold, everything is softer and more beautiful.
—NORMAN VINCENT PEALE

GRETCHEN

I didn't hear anything in church today. I sat beside Mom and Gloria and Marshall and thought of Kyle, prayed for Kyle, hoped for Kyle, and cried, feeling sorry for myself. I want him home. In one breath it scares me to death that he'll never be able to walk as he once did, but then in the next breath I'm grateful he's alive. In another breath I worry that he won't be able to do the work he loves, but as I exhale, I cry because he'll be able to hug Emma and Ethan each day.

I feel bad because I snapped at Melissa yesterday

and never apologized. I just couldn't hear about Ramona again. I couldn't take one more story about why Melissa's life is pathetic and how Ramona is to blame. The fact is, Melissa's life isn't pathetic. She not only works, but is able to keep a job and pay a mortgage, something her mother never did. Melissa's much smarter and brighter than she thinks she is; she could easily get a job in an office or even run her own business. I believe that. I need to apologize for snapping at her, but when we get home from church I'm exhausted and just want to take a nap. Some days are like that. For days and months on end I am mother, father, nurse, cook, maid, teacher, taxi driver, laundress, and referee. Every now and then I want to climb into bed without any responsibility and pull the covers over my head.

I throw on a pair of jeans and am putting on a sweatshirt when the doorbell rings. I groan because I don't want to see anyone. I open the door without looking through the peephole and scream. "Dad!"

"Hi, sweet pea." Tears pour over my cheeks as I throw my arms around his neck. He smells like shaving cream and cigars. "I'm here nine days early. Is that okay?" I nod and sob into the whiskers on his neck. The tears I hide from the kids so I won't

scare them pour over my father. "It'll be all right, Gretchen. Everything will be all right."

"I miss him so much, Dad."

He squeezes me tighter, and I'm eight years old again. "I know you do."

I try to hold it together but I can't; I'm a drippy mess. "Why are you here so early?"

"Because I thought you could use a break and maybe your old dad could give you one."

I laugh and cry at the same time. He's always known who I was. He's always known when I need to be quiet and when he needs to be quiet with me. He's always known when to pick me up and when I need to pick myself up. He's always known when I need a wink, a hug, a shoulder, or a time-out. My dad has his own brand of problems, but he still knows me. I pick up one of his bags and yell as I set it down in the entryway, shouting for the kids.

Dad is playing his fourth game with the kids (this time it's Battleship with Ethan) when the doorbell rings. I nearly laugh crossing to the door because I called Mom from my bedroom and asked her to come over for coffee. I didn't tell her Dad was here.

Sure, it was sneaky and maybe even a bit cruel, but I just had to do it. I swing the door open and smile. Her hair is perfect, and she's wearing a periwinkle scarf around her neck. She steps inside, and her eyes are the size of full moons when she screams. "Phillip!" She puts her hand on her forehead and I laugh, watching her. "I had no idea that you . . ." Her hand moves to her cheek and I laugh harder.

Dad is handsome as he smiles, standing to his feet. He is tall and his arms are well defined for a man his age. His hair is much thinner and grayer now, but his eyes are still as blue. "Look at you, Miriam," he says, crossing to her.

He kisses her cheek and Ethan laughs, slapping his forehead. "They can't kiss anymore. They're not married!"

Dad laughs and hugs Mom. She is stiff and gives me a dirty look. "You are an awful child, Gretchen Elizabeth."

Dad helps Mom take off her coat and he hangs it on the hall tree. "Relax, Miriam. She needs a good laugh."

"At the expense of her mother?!"

I take her gloves and purse. "I'm sorry, Mom. I just had to."

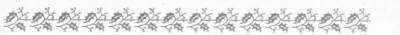

Mom straightens her hair and tries to peek at herself in the hall tree mirror. "I thought you were coming much later," she says, wiping something imaginary from her sweater.

Dad takes her hand and leads her to the sofa. "Sit down, Miriam. As I finish my game with Ethan I will tell you all about it."

"He came to surprise Mom," Ethan says.

Mom sits and straightens her slacks. "Well, good. We've all gotten a grand surprise today."

"D seven," Ethan says.

Dad makes the sound of an explosion and Ethan laughs. "You sank my battleship!" He looks at Mom and smiles. "You are a vision, Miriam."

Mom's face turns red and she swats at something in the air. "Oh, pish-posh applesauce. Be quiet, you!"

I laugh out loud from the kitchen because I've never heard my mother get flustered, but she doesn't know what to do with her hands and is grappling with the pillows on the sofa.

"No, no, you are," Dad says, sitting next to her. "It's like time forgot to march on with you."

I strain to hear them as I pour the coffee. "You look well, Phillip. It's good to see that you still have your hair and haven't gotten fat. You were quite

portly at Gretchen's graduation. You're not stooped over, your fingers aren't gnarled, and you're not gasping for breath so that's something, too."

I put some cookies on a plate and laugh out loud. She's dying out there. I walk to the living room with two cups of coffee in one hand and put them in front of Mom and Dad. That sounds so weird in my head. Mom and Dad. They each take a cup from me while Emma takes the cookies. I go back for my coffee and bring some cream and sugar. Something sweeps through my chest that feels like sadness or joy or maybe both. I don't know. I learned to live with the fact that my parents were no longer together, but here they are, sitting together and looking as I always imagined in my mind. Yet they're not together. I know that.

"Gretchen," Dad says. "Feel free to take off anytime to be with Kyle. Your mother and I can take care of the kids." I glance at Mom, waiting for her to protest the two of them working together, but she nods. "When are they moving Kyle to Texas?"

"On Tuesday."

He leans close to me on the couch and squeezes my leg. "Then why don't you book a plane ticket?" Tears fill my eyes and I nod. Dad wraps his arms

around me and kisses my cheek. "Why don't you give me a list of things you need done around here, okay?" He looks around the living room. "I'll start with hanging the pictures."

I cry, blowing my nose, and laugh. "I can't hang them like Kyle."

"I know, Gretch. Your mother never could hang a picture, either."

Mom groans and shakes her head. "She picked up all my horrible traits and all of your glorious ones!"

Dad wraps one arm around Mom and her back stiffens. "She clearly picked up on all of your beauty, Miriam."

"It is getting ever so deep in here," Mom says. "Where are my green Wellies when I need them most?"

"Maybe you can work on hooking up the DVD player, too, Dad. I hooked it up, but a line divides the screen somehow so the kids only see part of the picture."

He pulls my head onto his shoulder. "I will check into all electronics, and I will even plant some shrubs and a small tree out front. Now's the best time of year for that. It's the best time of year for so many things."

Thirteen

*Each of us is here for a brief sojourn; for what
purpose he knows not, though he senses it. But
without deeper reflection one knows from daily life
that one exists for other people.*

—ALBERT EINSTEIN

MELISSA

It's a cute two-story house with an enclosed porch
on the side. The smaller trees have Christmas lights,
and strands are wrapped around the shrubs in front
of the porch and outline the roof. I knock on the door
and feel my pulse knocking hard. A teenage boy answers wearing a white T-shirt and flannel pajama
pants. "Hi, is Karla home?"

"She and Dad and Gramps went to the hospital
already. Were you the lady who was bringing food?"

Crap. I didn't even think to bring anything. "No. I work with Josh at Wilson's. I just wanted to talk to your mom about your grandma."

"Grandma's here. Do you want to talk to her yourself?"

I feel the pulse on the side of my head. "Yeah. If she's up and doing okay. Josh told me she was sick."

He tips his head back and says, "Come on."

I follow him through a living room decorated in warm browns, plums, and gold, through a hallway, and then step down into a family room with a plush sofa and big, comfy chairs. There, in one of the chairs by the window is Josh's grandmother. "Grandma, this lady works with Josh." I hadn't told him my name, and he doesn't ask as he bolts from the room.

She turns to look at me and my eyes fill. Her hair is white and her full face is lined with wrinkles, but her eyes are as brown and openhearted as I remember. "Mrs. Schweiger," I say, choking on her name.

Her face opens in recognition and she puts something from her lap into a box on the table beside her. "Melissy!" She tries to stand and I move to her side, sitting down. She puts her hands on each side of my face and water covers her eyes. "Look at you! Look at what a beautiful woman you grew up to be!" It

feels like my throat is cracking, and streams of tears spill over my face. It's been close to thirty years since I've seen her, but all my life I've loved this woman as if she were my mother. She puts her arms around me and I crumble, remembering her hugging me as a child.

"I heard you were sick," I say, swiping at the tears on my face.

"I was sick, but now I'm much better."

"But you didn't go to the hospital this morning."

She shrugs her shoulders. "So this morning I'm not as better as I was yesterday." She sticks her finger up as if popping a balloon. "But tomorrow I'll be better than today. Eight years ago Albert and I moved to Albuquerque; the weather was supposed to be better for this and that ailment but look what happened. I got sick anyway." I love hearing her voice again and watching her gestures. "You are here." She makes it sound like she'd been expecting me. "Look at you. So beautiful. So smart. You were always so smart in school, bringing home those As in spelling and math. What do you do?"

"I just work in the mail room at Wilson's."

"What do you mean 'just'?" She looks at me and her face is solemn. "My Al just worked in the stock-

room at the supermarket until he managed the place one day. *Just* is nothing but a phony-baloney word. You're good enough to work in the mail room and smart enough to work your way out of it." She believes that, too. She reaches for the box on the end table and smiles. "I never stopped praying for you, Melissy." She takes the top off the box and pulls out a stack of photos. "I pick up each of these pictures in here everyday and I pray." She puts down a picture and names the person in the photo. "Josh, Eric, Taylor, Arianah, Drew, Taj, and Asia—my grandchildren. Karla, Mike, Madden, Grace, Louie, and Jen—my children and their spouses." She smiles at me. "And then all of my adopted children." She hands a photo to me, a picture of a kid about six or so standing in front of the old apartments where Ramona and I lived next door to the Schweigers. "Do you remember him? Bruce Linton from upstairs? Always had a runny nose?"

"Of course! He played with me and Louie everyday! Mean little kid."

She laughs. "He was spirited! He's the fire chief now somewhere in California. These . . ." She rummages through the photos until she finds one. "These were Bruce's parents. Remember?" I nod.

"Such nice people. His father died of a heart attack a couple of years ago, but his mother lives near Bruce." She puts another picture on my lap. "That's Rachel. She was Karla's age, so you might not remember her."

"She always wore her hair in a thick braid," I say, studying the picture.

"This was taken the day she got her hair cut. She's in Florida and is a fourth grade teacher." She flips through one picture after another. "That's Tommy. I don't know where he is. Garland lived next door to us after we moved away from the apartments. He works with computers. Ronnie is a policeman in Wyoming." On and on she went through a pile of worn photos of kids who wouldn't know her if they passed her on the street, but she prays for them anyway. She hands another picture to me, one of me when I was around nine, wearing green shorts and a striped yellow shirt and standing next to Karla, Madden, and Louie in front of a Ferris wheel at the county fair. "I saw your face every day. And I prayed for you." I look down at the photo and shake my head. "I prayed that God would protect you and guide you and your mother."

I look at her. "You remember what my mother

was like, Mrs. Schweiger, so I'm not sure if praying worked."

She lays her hand on top of mine, and her voice gets quiet. "I know life was hard for you at that time in the apartments, and I always prayed that you would be strong and that you wouldn't give up. I know that you haven't, because look at you! You're here and your heart pops right out of your eyes." She squeezes my hand and leans in close. "I know your mother must be proud of who you are."

"Ramona died less than two weeks ago."

The sound of air escaping her lungs fills the room, and she wraps her arm around the small of my back. "I'm so sorry, love." A single tear sneaks down my cheek and I brush it away with my finger. "How did she die?"

I search the floor for answers. "Alone in her apartment. Her heart stopped." I laugh. "I could have told the coroner that years ago!"

She rubs my back and leans over to the end table for the tissues, handing me two. "How was she at the end?"

I shake my head, trying to put it into words. "The same." It's all I can say about Ramona. "I feel awful—"

"Of course you do," she says, cutting me off.

I look at her. "No." My throat feels like it's clos-ing but I force the words through it. "I feel horrible because Ramona died and I feel free."

Her eyes are watery as she smiles, patting my hand. We sit in silence, and I know Mrs. Schweiger is trying to say something nice about Ramona but she's coming up blank. There is nothing to say about her. "You will have a place in your heart for your mother." I look at her. "You will. One day, someday, you will remember things and will store them away. You will love her in your own way." She squeezes my hand. "You always had so much love, Melissy."

Words clot together and form a ball in my throat. "You don't know me."

"I knew you as a child and I'm looking at you now." I feel a tear leak from my eye and snake down my cheek. Mrs. Schweiger dabs it with a tissue and pulls my head onto her shoulder. "I loved you like one of my own, Melissy." That makes me cry more, and I hold a tissue under my nose. "You were always such a special child." I haven't heard anything like this since I was a child inside her apartment, and I press the tissue into one eye and then the other. Mrs. Schweiger sits with me in the quiet and lets me

cry, rubbing my arm and patting my leg. "It is okay to feel free." I look up at her and she works at a smile. "You are not horrible. You're human."

I cover my eyes with the tissue. "This is the first time I've cried since she died."

She hands me two more tissues and pats my leg. "There will be more to come." She leans back and looks at me. "How did you know I was here?"

"I don't know," I say, wiping my face. "Josh works at Wilson's with me, and I don't think I ever paid attention when he was talking, but it all came together and made sense early this morning. I saw you and Karla yesterday as you got out of the elevator at the hospital, and this great sadness or something pushed down on me. I don't know what it was other than a great coincidence that I was leaving as you were getting there."

She smiles and lifts my picture from the top of the stack. "Or was it a finger snap from heaven letting you know to be aware and open your eyes?" I smile at her and she waves her hand in the air. "We pass everything off as coincidence. 'Eh, I needed more money to pay the rent and lo and behold I got paid more than I thought this week.' Or, 'I haven't worked in ten months. What a coincidence to run

into an old friend who needs help!' Or, 'I think I'll stop by Josh's house and ask if his old grandma is Mrs. Schweiger from the apartment days in Florida but what's this? It *is* her and she's actually sitting here talking to me.' Is it all coincidence or is it God's way of letting us know that we are heard and seen?"

I throw both hands in the air. "I give up!" She laughs and touches her head to my shoulder. I lean down and lift Ramona's note out of my backpack. "I suppose you'll say that my finding this in Ramona's apartment wasn't a coincidence, either?"

She puts on a pair of glasses that were sitting on the end table and reads the note, her eyes widening as she smiles. "This isn't a coincidence," she says, her voice getting louder. "This is destiny!"

It's midafternoon by the time I make it home. Mrs. Schweiger wanted me to stay and talk with Karla, Mike, and Mr. Schweiger when they got home from the hospital, but I could tell she was tired and needed to rest. I discovered that Karla and her husband moved to Grandon two years ago, when Mike got transferred and Mr. and Mrs. Schweiger visited them for a week last summer. I wonder if I passed

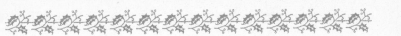

them in the car or saw them strolling through downtown? I'm smiling as I pull into my driveway and see Miriam's car at Gretchen's. It feels like I'm leaping as I run the length of sidewalk between our homes. I rap on the door to the rhythm of "Shave and a Haircut" and surprise myself. I've never done that before. Gretchen opens the door and I nearly burst inside. "You'll never believe what happened." I expect to see Miriam and I do, but she's sitting next to a man I don't know.

"This is my dad, Phillip," Gretchen says.

He stands and makes his way to me with his hand extended, but I take everyone off guard and hug him.

Gretchen laughs at the sight. "Are you drunk?"

"I'm so sorry," I say to Phillip. "I didn't mean to burst in but I just had to!"

"This is Melissa from next door. And she's never like this."

"I thought you were coming later," I say to Phillip.

"He was," Gretchen says. "But he came to help Mom with the kids so I can go to Texas." She looks at me with a wary eye. "Why are you acting weird?"

I tell them everything as we eat pizza for dinner, and I remember Mrs. Schweiger said she would call

about getting together with Karla tomorrow. I walk to my backpack and discover my phone is still on vibrate from my visit with her. There is a voice mail, and I hold the phone to my ear to listen. I feel the blood draining from my head and my legs turn to Jell-O as I walk back to the kitchen table. "Listen," I say, pressing the speakerphone button on my cell and holding it out at arm's length.

"Hey, Melissa, this is Jodi. I know it's Sunday and a weird day to call, but I really wanted to share this information with you. If you get this in the next hour, call me. If not, I'll be out of pocket the rest of the day. If I don't talk to you . . . well, I know you work at Wilson's in the morning, but if there's any time to come in in the morning, I think you should. We have some information on one of your siblings that Robert just discovered. A hospital called him back. I don't want to take up all your voice mail. Just drop in tomorrow morning if you're dying to know, or you can wait till you come in in the afternoon."

She left the message three hours ago while I was with Mrs. Schweiger, so I can't call her back.

Miriam is beaming, Phillip looks confused, and Emma says, "What's all that mean?"

"It means," Gretchen says, "that Melissa is about to meet one of her siblings."

I slept, but barely. It seems I woke up on the hour staring at the clock, anticipating and dreading the morning. Gretchen offered to go in with me when I talked to Robert and Jodi, but I didn't want to take her away from her dad, and I knew she needed to pack for her trip to Texas. I talked with my supervisor at Wilson's after I received the message from Jodi yesterday and told him I'd be in just as soon as I left the law office. My hands feel slippery on the wheel as I drive to the law office, and my chest feels like it's buzzing. I open the door and Jodi looks up from her desk, smiling. "You got my message," she says, coming into the entryway. I don't have time to respond. "Come on. Robert's here."

I follow her to Robert's office and feel nauseated or headachy, I'm not sure which. "I can't believe you already found one of them," I say.

"I told you that sometimes all it takes is one phone call." She uses the file in her hand to wave me into Robert's office and I walk past her. "The second sibling is proving problematic, but we're keeping at it."

Robert is at his computer and takes off his glasses when Jodi sets the file on his desk. He rubs his hands together and smiles. "So a sibling has been discovered! Are you ready to know?"

A sibling has been discovered. Never in my life did I think anyone would say those words to me. He bounces the file in the palm of his hand, a tiger pacing in its cage waiting for the door to open, waiting to be let go. I nod and he opens the cage.

Fourteen

*Miracles are a retelling in small letters of the very
same story which is written across the whole world
in letters too large for some of us to see.*
—C. S. LEWIS

GRETCHEN

I'm doing laundry when the phone rings. Dad took
Emma and Ethan to school and then said he was going to drop by the grocery store to stock up while I
was out of town. I don't even know what kind of
junk he's going to bring in for the kids. I can tell by
the connection on the other end that it's someone calling from Germany.

"Mrs. Daniels?" He doesn't need to tell me who
he is; I recognize that Texas drawl as Dr. Larimer.
Although he works at the Army Hospital and is a

career army doctor, I always found his accent to be so out of place in Germany. "Kyle needs another surgery," he says with a tone like "My buddy here needs more chips!" I try to figure in my mind how many surgeries Kyle's had already. Was it three or four?

"Do you remember the X-rays of Kyle's shoulder and face? The ones that looked like pieces of metal and rock were floating in midair?" I remember them as if I were staring at them now. "That area in the shoulder is called the brachial plexus." I imagine him using the tip of his pen and circling it above the X-ray as we talk. "It's basically a huge system of nerves that run from the spine to the arm. The shrapnel is floating. Over time, the shrapnel that is in Kyle's face will surface and make its way out." I want to ask how; wondering if it would swell to the surface like a pimple and eventually be squeezed out, but he continues to talk. "The shrapnel in his shoulder is getting dangerously close to this system of nerves, and our concern is that it will continue its way to the brachial artery, which could cause irreparable damage, even death. However, the surgery will slow his physical therapy because that arm will need to heal, but without it he could potentially lose

feeling or use of his arms if those nerves and arteries are compromised."

"So will they do that surgery when Kyle gets to
San Antonio?"

"We won't move him until we remove the shrapnel. We'll take him in today."

It registers what he's saying and it feels like he has
knocked the wind out of my lungs. "He's not coming
to the States?"

"Not at this time. In a few days. We'll keep you
up-to-speed."

It's shocking how your mind and emotions can
skyrocket and then plummet in seconds. When I
heard the connection on the phone and knew it was
someone in Germany calling, my thoughts were soar-
ing as I imagined Kyle coming home and the two of
us sitting together on the couch, watching the kids
open their presents before I moved to the kitchen to
cook my portion of Christmas dinner. Then all of us:
the kids, Mom, Dad, Melissa, and Kyle and me would
settle in at Gloria and Marshall's for Christmas dinner. Apparently, Dr. Larimer didn't receive my memo.

He hangs up before I can ask anything else and
I sit on the couch. Hot liquid sits on top of my eyes
and my chest tightens. My heart was set on seeing

Kyle tomorrow. I thought all his surgeries were behind him and all he had to do was focus on rehabilitation. I want him home! I'm so tired of not having him here with us. I pound the phone into the couch, yelling at no one and nothing or someone and everything. I am so angry and frustrated and tired. I dial Kyle's dad's cell number. He and Kyle's mom have been with him the entire time in Germany. They'll have more to say than the doctor, but the phone goes to voice mail. Do I fly to Germany again or wait for Kyle to get to Texas? How long will that be? I throw my head back on the couch and stew in the disappointment, tears, and unanswered questions.

When the doorbell rings I ignore it. Someone starts to knock and I remain still. I don't want to see anybody. The doorknob jiggles and I jump up, wondering if I locked the door. I see Melissa's head through the peephole and I feel like a louse pretending I'm not here. I open the door and see that she's holding a piece of paper and I know she must have the information about her sibling. She looks tired and pale, and I can only assume that she didn't sleep much last night. "Come on in."

"Are you okay?" she asks, crossing to the couch.

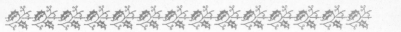

I shrug. "Kyle's not being moved to Texas tomorrow. He needs another surgery."

"For what?"

I slump down on the other end of the couch, not wanting to talk about it. "His arm. There's lots of shrapnel that's moving too close to the nerves and arteries."

"When *will* he fly to Texas?"

I shake my head, sighing. "A few days." We're both quiet and I know I've put a damper on her good news. If she has good news, that is. I'm hoping I can act thrilled for her when she tells me. "Well! Do you know the name of your sibling?"

She nods, the piece of paper quivering in her hand. She hands it to me and I strain to hear her. "I hoped it was you."

I stare at the names on the adoption document. Birth mother: Ramona McCreary. Adoptive father and mother: Phillip and Miriam Branch. I am shaking and can't breathe enough to find my voice. Ever since I was a teenager my parents told me I could find the woman who gave me up for adoption, but I never wanted to; I genuinely never *wanted* to. As far as I was concerned I had my parents. "I . . ." I look at Melissa and she's as shaken as I am. Her pale,

perplexed face makes me laugh out loud and I fall back into the couch cushions. "You look like I feel!"

She watches me laugh, and her baffled look makes me laugh harder. "This is how you respond?" She picks up one of the throw pillows and whacks me with it several times. "And I thought I was the one who got the socially backward gene. Obviously, it was you!"

I howl louder with a sense of relief and excitement and look at Melissa, my eyes filling. It's one thing to get a package in the mail that you didn't expect or to hear the voice of an old high school friend on the phone who happens to be in town and wants to catch up over coffee. Those are nice, make-your-day surprises. Getting a sister you never knew existed is a bolt from the blue bombshell. It's a voice from the wings telling you to take your mark because the next act is going to be a doozy. Somewhere along the way I went from barely tolerating Melissa to missing her when she wasn't around. Maybe that's how it is for sisters. I throw my arms around her; it's the first time I've hugged her, and I laugh again because I'm hugging my sister.

I'm not sure if we're laughing or crying, but we stay tangled together until I sniff so loud that she

pulls away, holding her ear. The weight of what has happened fills my living room, and we stare at the names on the paper that were typed by some unnamed secretary thirty-seven years ago. Did she know then, as she pecked each letter on her typewriter that lives would collide someday? Did Ramona ever think about it? Probably not, given what I know about her. "Why did you say you hoped it was me? Did you know I was adopted?"

Melissa nods. "Gloria told me the first day I met her and your mom. Yesterday when I heard Jodi's voice mail I immediately hoped that they found my sister and that she was you. It was a stupid, crazy thing to hope for because the chances of that happening were zero."

"Or one hundred percent!"

Melissa and I run to Mom's door and burst through without knocking. I called Dad and told him to go to her house right away, and Mom called Gloria. All I said was that I had news for them.

Mom and Dad never met the woman who gave birth to me, never even caught a glimpse of her; that's the story they always told me. They took me home

the day I was born, and when the time was right they told me I was adopted. I know Mom worried that somehow I'd be scarred, left with this big birth mother wound in my heart, but it never worked that way with me. Ramona was a woman who carried me to delivery and "handed me over," so to speak, to my parents. She wasn't my mom.

Mom is handing Dad a cup of coffee when Melissa and I stampede into her kitchen. "Sit down!" I say. "You have to sit down."

Gloria moves to a chair. "Lord have mercy. The last time I heard that, the doctor told me I was pregnant again!"

Mom, Dad, and Gloria are sitting at the table looking at us, their faces wondering and open and beautiful with age. "Kyle needs another surgery and won't be flying to Texas tomorrow, which means I won't be flying to Texas, either."

Mom looks confused. "And you're excited about this?"

"I can't even tell you how angry and disappointed and sad I am about this."

Gloria crosses her arms. "In Georgia we always had a different way of expressing those emotions."

"I know!" I say, my voice lifting like fireworks. "I

am *sooo* disappointed!" The looks on their faces make Melissa and me laugh out loud, and Mom shakes her head. "You always told me to find the woman who gave birth to me, right?"

Mom nods. "And now you're going to?"

"I don't have to. Her oldest daughter found me."

The three of them sit for a moment, letting it sink in. Mom's hands attack each side of her face and she lets out a little squeak, her eyes shifting from me to Melissa. We're both grinning like cats and she rises, dazed, to her feet. "Melissa . . ."

Gloria's hands flap in front of her. "Are you kidding us?"

Melissa shakes her head and Dad pounds the table. Melissa lays the adoption document on the table, and Gloria, Mom, and Dad read it out loud, their voices mounting together as each name is read. "Where are those Action News people when you need them?" Gloria asks, hugging Melissa.

Mom holds the document and studies it closer. "So you have the same mother, but do they know . . ."

"We don't have the same mother, Miriam," Melissa says. "My mother was Ramona, and Gretchen's gestational carrier was Ramona. She had a different mother. A good mother." Mom purses her lips

together and puts a hand on the side of her face. "I never knew the man involved in my entry, and given the fact that Gretchen and I are two years apart and Ramona never stayed with a man for longer than a week . . . the odds are low the same man was involved. That would be out of character for Ramona."

Mom looks dazed and seems to be taking this harder than I imagined.

"Marshall hasn't left for the store yet," Gloria says. "Would you come tell him, Melissa?"

"I told my supervisor that I'd be at work after I left the law office. Now look where I am!"

Gloria puts her hand on Melissa's elbow. "This is the perfect excuse for your supervisor. Tell him you were at the owner's house!"

There are some things I know about Gloria, and one is that there's no way she'd ever leave a good party unless there was an urgent need, like she was about to throw up or saw that her best friend was about to throw up. I know she saw Mom's face, and because she knows Mom so well she wanted to give her room. The door closes behind them, and I sit down at the table, tapping it so Mom and Dad will sit back down, too. "So, what do you think, Mom?"

She holds the paper and shakes her head. Miriam

Lloyd-Davies is stumped and stupefied. "I . . ." Her voice is searching for the words. "I . . . just never imagined such a thing happ—" She puts her hand on her head and looks at Dad.

"It's unbelievable," he says. "You have a sister! The kids have a new aunt! Kyle has a sister-in-law, and the way I see it, we have another daughter!"

Mom doesn't react and I get out of my chair, squatting down next to her. I haven't had much time to think about what has just happened, but in a fleeting moment I realize I stood at the graveside of the woman who gave birth to me, a woman who I would most likely never want to invite over for dinner or even chat with in line at the grocery. I'm sad that Ramona never appreciated Melissa or the trees and sky, the bright, hollow beak of a toucan or a patch of wildflowers. I'm sad that her life is over before she ever lived it. "You know, sometimes you just have to point out the obvious." Mom looks at me and waits. "No doubt about it. I got the better end of that deal."

I finally get through to Kyle's dad, and he gives the phone to Kyle. "Hi, Gretch." I laugh out loud, crying,

so excited to hear his voice and to tell him what has happened. His voice sounds stronger, but the words still take longer to come out. We'll talk about his surgery coming up in two hours and whether I should come to Germany or wait until he flies to Texas. I know we'll get to all that, but I'm about to pop. "Are you laughing or crying?" he asks.

"Both!" I yell into the phone. "Something amazing has happened!"

"Really? On a scale of one to ten, how amazing is it?"

"A thousand and twenty!"

Fifteen

Small deeds done are better than great deeds planned.

—PETER MARSHALL

MELISSA

I picked up Mrs. Schweiger yesterday afternoon and took a bag of jalapeño chips to Josh in the hospital. Mr. Schweiger answered the door looking bald and much shorter than I remembered. His eyes nearly disappeared when he smiled and latched on to me with the strength of someone years younger. They were always so good together, these two with their fine German stock and sensible ways.

Before we left for the hospital I relived Jodi's voice mail for them about finding my sibling, and they sat on the edge of their chairs as if I was the

most interesting storyteller they'd ever heard. When I told them my sibling turned out to be the woman next door to me, Mrs. Schweiger threw her hands in the air and yelled something in German. "It was destiny!" she says, holding both my hands. "I told you it was destiny!" Her eyes are watery as she looks at me. "You could have gone your whole life and never known your sister, but your mother wanted you to know that."

"Not really. If we hadn't found the note in her apartment I would have never known."

She pats my hand too hard. "You don't know that. She wrote the note. She wanted you to know. She was trying to do the right thing for you." She is nodding, waiting for me to believe. Although she and my mother said very little to each other the three years we lived next to them and Mrs. Schweiger would have no reason to defend her, I know that she saw something in Ramona that only another mother can see.

"I know," I say, believing her.

I don't have to be at Wilson's until ten this morning and decide to do some laundry when I hear voices

outside. I move the blinds and see Phillip and Miriam standing in the yard, so I open the door, folding my arms against the cold. Miriam is wearing a long camel-colored coat with black leather gloves and a furry hat, and Phillip wears a red-and-black-checked coat with a Pittsburgh Steelers hat. "Morning!" I yell, waving.

Phillip gestures for me to come closer. "Melissa! Come decide for us." I reach for my coat out of the closet and close the door. Five shrubs sit in black plastic tubs near the front of the condo. "I was trying to plant these this morning, but Miriam dropped in to boss me around and tells me I have them all wrong."

"I did not say that Phillip. I said if that's how you want to order them, then fine, but I wouldn't do it that way."

"I apologize. My translation was way off," he says, looking at her. "Melissa? What will look good? Those three are heather laurels and these two are azaleas. I thought the azaleas would be a good background for the laurels."

Miriam is shaking her head, and the way the fur on her hat moves around it looks like something alive is on her head. "You don't put a flowering shrub

behind a big green thing, Phillip. You put the green and then the shorter flower bush in front of it."

"Azalea," he says.

"Whatever! You don't put the thing of beauty behind a wall of green."

Phillip looks at me for help. "She's right," I say, sheepish.

Miriam gives Phillip a smug eye roll. "When you told me you were going to do this I just knew that I must come here to see that this is done properly."

"Where's Gretchen?" I ask.

"She dropped the kids off at school and was going to two different dental offices that are looking for hygienists," Phillip says. "One is thirty minutes away. I told her to eat lunch out and enjoy the day. I'm hoping I can get this done while she's gone."

Miriam marches to the door. "I'm going to find some proper clothes. I'm sure Gretchen has several grubby things I can wear."

Phillip is digging out the old shrubbery, which is so small and dead that it can practically be pulled up rather than dug, while I prepare the empty holes for the new plants when Miriam opens the front door. Even in Gretchen's "grubby" clothes she looks like a

million bucks. "Besides his poor design judgment, Phillip has always had a green thumb. We had yard of the year one year. When was that, Phillip?"

"In '72," he says. "Miriam picked out all the plants and flowers. She's always had an eye for beauty. Beauty attracts beauty, though."

Gretchen would laugh watching Miriam's face turn flame red. I keep my head down as I help pull out another dead shrub so they won't see me grinning.

"People slowed down just to see our yard," Miriam says, pouring some bagged soil and fertilizer into a hole.

"Half the time they were slowing down to look at Miriam," Phillip says, serious as a news report.

Miriam laughs and reaches for some peat moss. "Oh, Phillip, really!"

"I can see that, Miriam," I say, loosening a heather laurel from the plastic container.

She laughs again and Phillip leans on his shovel. "People are still slowing down to look at her. Just look there."

Miriam and I turn behind us to see the mailman in his car. "The mail carrier!" Miriam says. "Do be quiet, Phillip."

"Look at him! He can't take his eyes off you."

Miriam laughs harder than I've ever seen her, and she uses her trowel to swipe at Phillip's leg. If I didn't know better, I would say they're getting along. I would say they're teasing each other, flirting even!

By the time I leave for Wilson's, Phillip and Miriam are heading inside Gretchen's for a coffee break, and something tells me the shrub planting might take them all day.

For the first time in years I look forward to going to work. The streets and storefronts seem to have their own energy. They're pulsing or buzzing or ringing out some melody that I've never been able to hear before, and thoughts rush through my mind. Ramona. Gretchen. Josh. Mrs. Schweiger. Layton and Associates. "We pass everything off as coincidence," Mrs. Schweiger had said. I stop at the square and look at the gazebo and the three decorated fir trees. Why would anyone take such effort to make those trees beautiful? Why would anyone go to so much trouble? Something in my chest catches and I swear I hear a finger snap from heaven.

. . .

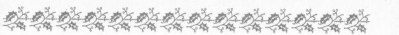

Before I clock out at Wilson's, Jodi calls from the law office and says the computers are down. Since that's the bulk of my work there, she tells me to take the day off, which I'm happy to oblige! I race home and smile at the sight. Phillip and Miriam are in my yard planting what looks like the last of some new shrubs. For the first time since I've known her, Miriam looks worn and ruffled. I get out of the car, grinning. "What are you two doing?"

"One condo couldn't look that good and this one look horrible," Phillip says. "So we went and bought some matching shrubs."

"But I . . ."

Phillip puts his arm around my shoulder. "Just so you know. This is my gift to our newest family member."

"I never know what to say," I say, frustrated with myself. "This is so great!" I hug them both and stand looking at them. "Will you both help me with something?" Honest to goodness, I've never had a brainstorm before. Seriously, I haven't. But this is a good one and it's bigger than me.

Sixteen

Out of difficulties grow miracles.
—JEAN DE LA BRUYÈRE

GRETCHEN

I never thought I'd see the day that my parents were actually working side by side together again, but Melissa swore to me that they planted the shrubs together Tuesday, and on Wednesday Mom and Dad came for the kids and me and we went shopping for a Christmas tree after school. The kids stayed up too late decorating it, but I didn't mind. I found myself standing back and watching Mom and Dad with Ethan and Emma. Dad's always had the ability to be so silly with children, and Mom would laugh out loud at his lousy jokes and poor impersonations.

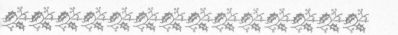

When the tree was decorated we took pictures in front of it: just the kids, the kids with Mom, the kids with Dad, the kids with Mom and Dad, the kids with me, and me with Melissa. It felt so strange to pose for a picture with her because in a way it felt as if we'd always done it.

Kyle called on Thursday and said that doctors still hadn't told him when they'd move him to Texas. His surgery was successful on Monday, so I couldn't figure out why they just didn't move him. I wanted to come to Germany but Kyle wouldn't hear of it. "You'll just get here and they'll transfer me. Just wait until they decide to move me and then come to Texas." Although my parents are here and I have the kids and Melissa, this faraway feeling is getting worse as Christmas gets closer.

The kids got out of school for Christmas break on Friday, and since then they've managed to tear through our house and Mom's like crazy people. Tonight is the chamber orchestra concert and benefit for Glory's Place. Gloria has been in the newspaper and on the local radio station soliciting anyone and

everyone to help Bake a Difference for Glory's Place. Melissa even baked in her own oven! She brought over a chocolate cake yesterday and was beaming as she set it on the table. "That actually looks good enough to eat," I said.

I haven't seen much of her in the past few days because of her work schedule, but we've spent time in the evening trying to find similar toes or hands, ears or kneecaps, but have come up with few resemblances. She's tall and I'm short. Her face is angular and mine is round. Her fingers are long with soft fingernails and mine are short with hard fingernails. Dark hair sits on her head and blond strands cover mine. She is abrupt and I am deliberate, but hopefully I'll teach her how to be more measured and she'll teach me how to speak freely.

Dad and Melissa went to church with us this morning. Dad's never been a church man, but he's always open to it at Christmas, especially when he's with his grandkids. Melissa's been to church a few times when she was a kid, with the Schweigers but never with Ramona or on her own. She was still as she listened to the reading from Luke and wiped

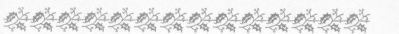

her eyes when all the children sang "O Holy Night"
and "Hark! The Herald Angels Sing." I cried, too,
and I caught Dad rubbing his eyes. For Kyle's first
tour of Afghanistan the soldiers sang "Silent Night"
together on Christmas Day, and Kyle said nobody
dared look at one another because there wasn't a
dry eye in the whole bunch. Seems like the songs
of Christmas have the same effect no matter where
you are in the world. I cried through the entire service again.

Two days ago, Gloria asked Melissa and me if
we'd help set up for Bake a Difference at the community center. We eat a quick lunch with Dad and
the kids before driving across town to the civic
center. The chamber orchestra is already in place
practicing on stage as Mom, Gloria, Melissa, and I
set up tables in the lobby. Gloria hands me a tightly
rolled banner. "Could you figure a way to hang this,
babe?"

"What does it say?" I ask.

"Bake a Difference. And right under that in letters that look like gingerbread it says, 'To Benefit
Glory's Place.'"

"Don't you think if people see all these baked

goods that they're going to know it's a bake sale, Gloria?" Mom asks, flapping a tablecloth out in front of her.

Gloria helps her smooth out the tablecloth. "This is not just a bake sale, Miriam! People all over this community have been baking a difference! Do you see Rice Krispies treats here? Brownies? Overbaked cookies? Saran Wrap, for crying out loud?" Mom hangs her head, waiting for Gloria to finish. "No. That's because this is not your run-of-the-mill bake sale. We have boxes and ribbons and bows! This is an event!"

Mom looks down at herself. She's wearing black slacks with a red chenille sweater and a strand of pearls. "I don't know what I was thinking. I always wear an evening gown to an event."

"I was hoping you'd go home and change," Gloria says, winking at me.

Mom's eyes are ablaze. "You are wearing a sweatshirt with a mouse dressed like Santa Claus, Gloria!"

"Don't worry. I got you one for Christmas."

Mom flaps her hand in the air as if brushing Gloria away, and Melissa and I work on figuring a way to hang the banner. A steady stream of women

and men come into the lobby throughout the afternoon, delivering their baked goods, and as they do, Gloria makes a beautifully handwritten card for each one stating what it is. There is every imaginable cake: coconut, pistachio, chocolate rum, red velvet, white chocolate, cranapple, banana pecan, lemon, spice, apple, German chocolate, and more! There are yule logs, truffles, caramels, a chocolate hazelnut soufflé, pecan torts, pumpkin cream and cranberry tarts, a tower of cupcakes, countless cheesecakes that could be on the cover of *Bon Appétit*—pumpkin, toffee, gingerbread, eggnog, persimmon, turtle, and cherry amaretto—and a string of pies that could be displayed in any bakery: sweet potato, chocolate pecan, sour cream raisin, apple cheddar, orange meringue, lemon meringue, mincemeat, coconut custard, cherry crumble, caramel, and pear. But Gloria didn't just write "apple" or "coconut" on each card. She wrote, "Apple Bliss Cake" or "Coconut Dream Pie." Mom ripped up the card that said "Banana Bonzo Cake" because she said that anything with the word *bonzo* in it should not be taken seriously. She wanted Gloria to call it Banana Surprise Cake, but Gloria said she wouldn't want to be surprised by a banana. They settled on Decadent Banana Cake.

An older woman holds on to the arm of a middle-aged woman and delivers a cake. Melissa sees them and grabs my arm, pulling me toward them. "Mrs. Schweiger! You baked a cake!"

"When has she not baked?" the other woman says.

So this is Mrs. Schweiger? She wraps her arms around me and then holds me out by the shoulders, looking at me. "I know who you are," she says. "You're Gretchen."

"This is Mrs. Schweiger and Karla," Melissa says.

"I figured that out."

Mrs. Schweiger continues to eyeball me, and then she hugs me to her again. "I need your picture," she says.

"Okay. What kind of picture?"

"A family picture."

"It's been a while since we've taken a family picture, but I'll get one to you. I could e-mail one when we have one taken again."

She holds on to my hand and squeezes. "I don't do the e-mail. I need a picture for my box."

"Her box of prayers," Melissa says. "You're going in the box." I don't know exactly what that means but

have a feeling that Melissa's picture spent more time out of Mrs. Schweiger's box than in it.

When Dalton and Heddy arrive from Glory's Place we all work together placing each cake and confection into a box donated by Betty's Bakery and then wrapping it with a ribbon and bow.

Everything is in place at five o'clock, and we stand back and look at the tables. I have to admit that when Gloria first talked about baking a difference, I never thought of it turning out looking this good. She runs to her bag and pulls out prices she has slipped inside picture frames.

Mom bends her head to read one sign. "Beginning donation of fifty dollars per baked good! Are you crazy, Gloria? Who's going to pay fifty dollars for a pie?"

"They're not paying fifty dollars for a pie, Miriam. If they wanted a pie they'd go buy one at Betty's for twelve bucks. They're donating to a cause."

Mom shakes her head. "What in the world are we going to do with all these cakes and pies?"

Dad drops the kids off an hour before the doors are supposed to open. Emma and Ethan take their

place behind the tables to help Mom sell, and I
know they'll be doing more playing than working,
but Mom gives me a look that says she has it all under
control.

I am in front of the tables and arranging a stack
of cakes when the audience begins to fill the lobby.
Dalton and Heddy take charge as Gloria and Mom
have disappeared, and I realize Melissa isn't nearby,
either. A man writes a check to Glory's Place for one
hundred dollars for the Captivating Cherry Cream
Cheese Cake, and I hand the box to him when I hear
a voice somewhere behind me.

"Do you have any Snickers bars?"

Did he say a candy bar?

"How about popcorn?"

Can't he see we aren't a concession stand? I
want to laugh, but the voice pounds at my heart and
I turn around, screaming. The kids fly out from
behind the table and slam into Kyle. I can't move
because I can't feel my legs. Is it really him? Is he
here? He's wearing Kyle's fatigues, so it looks like
him, but I can't think straight. Kyle is in Germany.
A man and woman in front of me step aside, and I see
Emma crying and gripping her dad around his waist.
Ethan is jumping up and down, and I don't think I'm

breathing. Kyle uses some sort of crutch and walks toward me with Emma attached to him, and I fall into his shoulder. It is him. I reach my arms around him and try to say something, but it's all lodged in the back of my throat. If people are around us, I don't hear them. I don't even know where I'm at anymore.

Mom is a mess as she reaches for Kyle. "Welcome home, Kyle," she says. "We are all so grateful to have you back. You just have no idea."

Melissa is videotaping the whole thing, and I signal for her to come closer. "This is . . ." I say, but it comes out in squeaks.

"This is Melissa," Kyle says, looking at her. "The brand-new sister and event coordinator."

Melissa's eyes are smiling and she hugs Kyle; this part of the video is going to look like a train wreck. "Welcome home," she says.

Mom smiles, with her arm looped through Kyle's. "It was Melissa's idea to call the doctors in Germany to see if there was any way Kyle could come home for Christmas." I look at Melissa and she shrugs, barely smiling. "Your dad called Tom and Alice." She points to the side, and I see Kyle's parents, stepping toward us. "They talked to the doctors. And here is Kyle."

"You mean everyone knew about this?"

"Not everybody," Kyle says, pulling me into his side. "The hard part was keeping you from booking a plane ticket to Germany or Texas!"

I'm still so confused. "When do you have to go to San Antonio?"

"I don't. The doc says I can do physical therapy right here."

I can't keep the tears off my face, and someone finally hands me a tissue. Gloria and Marshall sweep in next to us and introduce themselves to Kyle, then Robert and Kate Layton and Betty Grimshaw from Betty's Bakery. Word buzzes through the lobby of what happened and people I've never met in Grandon take the time to welcome Kyle home and thank him for his service. Mrs. Schweiger pulls a small camera out of her purse and holds it to her eye. "Smile," she says. Several of us are clumped together for the photo, but I don't think it matters to her. The picture's going straight into the box. On and on people come to clap Kyle on the shoulder or shake his hand. Parents look at their children and say, "This man just got back from serving our country," hoping they'll understand, and some do, but most don't know what that means.

A woman from the chamber of commerce leads us to seats at the front that have been reserved for our family. Ethan sits on Kyle's lap and Emma leans over onto his chest, wrapping her arms around him while I hold his hand. We're just one big pile of flesh waiting for the concert to begin. Mom and Dad and Kyle's parents are with us, along with Gloria, Marshall, Melissa, and the Schweigers. I try my best to capture their faces in my mind, hoping I'll always remember, but I'm afraid much of this night will be a blur.

Adam Clark, the chamber president walks to the front of the stage and greets the audience and tells a little about the Bake a Difference fund-raiser for Glory's Place. In the next breath he looks at Kyle and welcomes him home. "He was wounded in September in Afghanistan and just got here today." The place erupts in applause and whoops, and everybody is on their feet cheering. Kyle lifts his hand to wave, but I know he is embarrassed. I've never met a man or woman yet in the military who serves for this sort of thing; it's just not in them. "Kyle and Gretchen and their two children chose Grandon as their new home for when Kyle finished his service

in the army." More applause and I feel Kyle's hand clamping harder on mine. "So the welcome wagon has been busy. Well, Melissa has been busy," he says, looking through the crowd of faces for her. Melissa's not looking at me, afraid of what that will mean to her emotions, I suppose. The same woman from the chamber who showed us to our seats hands me a basket of cards. "Businesses in the community responded to your coming home, Kyle, and you'll find discounts to Wilson's, free meals at Betty's Bakery, oil changes and tire rotation and balance at City Auto Service, passes to Jump World for the kids, a new deck that will be built onto your home courtesy of James Lumber, painting the interior of your home donated by Three Guys and a Paintbrush, and lots of other things to say thank you and welcome!" The music begins with "Sleigh Ride" and Kyle's grip on my hand finally relaxes.

Gloria waves me away from the tables when I come back at intermission to help. Mom, Melissa, Dalton, and Heddy work alongside her, and Dad gives me a thumbs-up. The fund-raiser for Glory's Place is going to be a success. Money adds up fast when someone

pays one thousand dollars for Wonderland White Chocolate Cake or Visions of Sugar Plum Pie.

Kyle and the kids and I leave after intermission. Kyle is exhausted, and in truth, he just wants to be home, to see it for the first time, and tuck the kids in bed, our bed. We all pile in it together and look through the gift cards and certificates to businesses I wasn't even familiar with yet, strangers who are blessing us. Melissa solicited Mom and Dad, and they spread out across town, visiting businesses and telling them about Kyle. We open haircut certificates and free movie passes, massages and lawn mowing, weekend trips to a bed-and-breakfast and a vacation package to Florida. On and on they go and I try to envision Melissa taking charge of this, of her and Mom and Dad fanning across town to talk to local businesses. It seems impossible that that woman is the same woman we moved next door to, but like I said, she's smarter than she thinks.

Kyle falls asleep listening to the kids tell him everything from how Micah at school can put a spaghetti noodle in his nose and pull it out of his mouth to why pink is no longer Emma's favorite color. The kids doze off soon afterward, and I watch them all, touching Kyle again to make sure he's really with us.

My insides are still shaking in the dark, and I don't know if it's from feeling grateful or overwhelmed. I know so many others have come home from a tour of duty and have not been offered a free car wash, let alone a word of appreciation. They come home and work themselves back into a community without much of a rustle one way or the other. It's what I expected, but sometimes the unexpected can really take a bite out of expectations. I reach across Ethan, who is breathing heavy in sleep, lay my hand on Kyle's chest, and close my eyes.

Seventeen

At the touch of love, everyone becomes a poet.
—PLATO

MELISSA

I've never done anything for anybody and that's the truth. I've lived inside myself, which is a pretty lonely and depressing place for thirty-nine years and I wanted out. I was scared to death when I walked into businesses in town and asked if they could do something to welcome Kyle home. Phillip and Miriam went with me on the first two visits, and then we branched out on our own. There was something mischievous, something that felt like electricity beneath my skin, in keeping this a secret from Gretchen and the kids. I went in earlier each morning

to Wilson's, and Robert gave me three days off so I could "work the streets" as Gloria said.

I replay the image of Kyle walking through the civic center doors and watching Gretchen, unaware of his presence and helping someone buy a cake for the fund-raiser. Phillip was grinning and Miriam was crying. For the rest of my life I'll remember Gretchen's scream and her face. It was the best night of my life.

The roll of wrapping paper I bought two days ago is on the kitchen table and I open it. I haven't purchased a Christmas gift in years, so I never had a use for wrapping paper. Gloria helped me find a gift for Miriam: trouser socks. They sounded boring, but Gloria said nothing brings a smile to Miriam's face like a good pair of trouser socks, so I bought her three pairs. I'm giving Phillip cigars, Emma a game that the lady in the toy department at Wilson's said was popular, Ethan a football, and Kyle some gloves and a new winter hat to keep his head warm.

I pick up Gretchen's gift and stare at it; it's a frame that says "sisters" at the top with a photo of us together in front of her Christmas tree, and below it is the note she found in Ramona's apartment. I had it mounted and framed in town, and since I've

picked it up, I can't stop looking at it. What if Kyle and Gretchen had decided to move closer to his parents rather than Miriam? What if Ramona's landlord had left the message about her death with someone else on the street or given up altogether? If one thing, however small, would have been different, I would have never known Gretchen as my sister and I doubt I ever would have known her as my neighbor. I would have just stayed behind my closed door and wished she and her children would do the same. If I strain, I swear I can hear that finger snap from heaven again.

Once I finish wrapping the presents I grab a cup of coffee and a piece of Mrs. Claus Coffee Cake I bought last night and head to work. Wilson's will be swamped today with last-minute shoppers.

My cell phone rings at one when I'm on break and I assume it's Gretchen because she wants me at her house after work for Christmas Eve dinner at six. I know she's calling to pester me again about how to make pistachio salad. It's pudding, marshmallows, pineapple, and Cool Whip! How hard can it be? I muster up a spring in my voice because she says I always sound grumpy when I answer the phone.

"Melissa, it's Robert." He's been out of the law

office since Monday; his grandchildren are in town.
My heart skips a beat, wondering if he has news.
"It was a great night last night. You did tremendous
work."

"Thanks, Robert," I say, putting a dollar bill inside the slot of the vending machine. "Gretchen and
her kids were surprised."

"They were," he says. "And if you're ready, I have
one for you." My heart starts that wild beating again
as I bend down and pull out a bag of pretzels. "I received a call about your brother." I'm smiling and
flop down on a chair in the break room. "Are you
ready?"

"Yes."

"He took a bit longer to track down because the
name his adoptive mother used on his adoption
papers was her stepfather's name and not her birth
name. That stepfather's name tracked to several men
with the same name, and long story short, we finally
tracked her back to her birth name and came up
with a little boy born in 1976 to Ramona McCreary
and adopted by Les and Susan Linton." My mind is
racing as I try to write all this down on the back of
a magazine lying on the table. "I have Bruce's information if you want it." I scribble everything down

on the magazine and take a breath before I thank
Robert and hang up the phone.

I dial Gretchen's cell but it goes to voice mail. I
don't leave a message because I want to tell her in
person. I feel as nervous this time around as I did
when Robert told me he'd discovered my sister. The
names Les and Susan Linton bounce off my brain as
I eat the pretzels, and I keep staring at their names
written on the back of the magazine. I try calling
Gretchen's home and cell numbers again before I go
back to work, but both phones go to voice mail. I put
the magazine in my locker and try to keep my mind
busy for the remainder of the afternoon, but it's like
putting a piece of candy in front of a kid and telling
him not to touch it for four more hours.

The afternoon is busy and goes fast, and the names
Les and Susan Linton continue to roll through my
mind. At four thirty, I'm organizing the mail room
when a face pops into my mind and my pulse surges.
I run upstairs to the break room and roll through the
combination on the lock and yank open my locker,
snatching the magazine off the top shelf. I read the
names again, feeling my heart in my throat.

I run out the door and ask every employee in
sight if they've seen my supervisor, Pat. "He was in

the office," the lady in jewelry, whose name I never can remember, says.

I take the stairs by two and fling open the office door. He's standing at the copy machine. "Pat!" He turns and sees me standing with the door open. "Something huge has come up. I'm off in thirty. Can I go now?"

"How huge is it?" he asks, smiling.

"I'm going to be a sister!"

He looks confused but waves his hand in the air. "Go! Have a great Christmas." I'm yelling the same thing to him as I bolt down the stairs and grab my coat and backpack from my locker and clock out.

I can feel my heart beating high in my chest as I ring the doorbell. Karla opens the door and smiles. "Merry Christmas!" I say. "I hope I'm not bothering you on Christmas Eve."

She steps aside. "Get in here! Mom and I were having some coffee and some of the cake I bought last night. Want some?"

"Which one did you buy?" I ask, following her to the kitchen.

"Frosting the Snowman."

I laugh at another one of Gloria's names. "What kind is that?"

"White," she says, which makes me laugh harder.

Mrs. Schweiger is at the kitchen table with her box of photos sitting on top of it, so I know she's already been busy today. The kitchen smells yummy and I wonder why they're having cake so close to dinnertime. "Cake before dinner?" I say.

"Mom has to have something on her stomach for her medicine," Karla says. "I said, 'how about some cheese and crackers' and she said, 'how about some cake?' You see who won."

I hug Mrs. Schweiger, and she cuts a slice of cake for me while Karla sets a cup of coffee in front of me. "I don't need any cake," I say.

"It's Christmas. You do out-of-ordinary things at Christmas and wear big pants."

That makes me laugh and I take a bite. "Mrs. Schweiger," I say, getting right to it. "Do the names Les and Susan Linton sound familiar?"

Her eyes are big and she smiles. "From the apartments. Of course. They were wonderful people. Very kind."

"Did you know much about them?" She opens her mouth to answer, but I rephrase what I said. "Did you ever suspect or imagine anything about them?"

She leans forward, looking at me and I see

something in her eyes. She points her finger at me, grinning. "What are you up to, Melissy?"

I smile. "I think you know." Karla looks from me to her mother and waits.

"It would have only been a thought," says Mrs. Schweiger.

"And what was that thought?"

"I knew how their family was brought together. They were always very open about adopting all their children."

"What else?" I ask, taking another bite of Frosting the Snowman cake.

"You and your mother had already lived at the apartments nearly three years when I saw Ramona watching the little Linton boy play one day in the parking lot. You remember how the children would play tag in that big, circular end of the lot. Your mother *never* stopped to watch the children, but that day she did, and as she looked at him, I looked at her and then back at him, trying to see what she was looking at. Something jiggled somewhere in my brain, and I didn't know what to think by what I was seeing but noticed that your mother was upset." She pats my hand. "In the couple of weeks following, all I could do was try to steal a glance of Ramona from

time to time and look at that little boy and wonder, but I never knew anything for sure." She pulls out the stack of photos from her box and flips through them.

I lean back in my chair. "That's why Ramona moved out of there so fast, isn't it? She knew that the Linton boy was the little boy she'd given up for adoption."

Mrs. Schweiger's mouth puckers and she cocks her head. "I think she suspected. And long after you left, I always wondered."

"And the Lintons?"

"They never knew Ramona. Never even saw her, as far as I know."

I hand her the magazine. "My boss just located my brother. His name is Bruce Linton."

Karla says, "Are you kidding?" and tears fill Mrs. Schweiger's eyes.

"His parents are Les and Susan Linton."

Mrs. Schweiger lets out a whoop and plops Bruce's picture down in front of me.

"And he's a fire chief in California!"

There's no time to make pistachio salad, but I hope everyone will forgive me, considering I've been a bit

busy tracking down my brother! I forget to knock and walk into Kyle and Gretchen's, holding up the magazine. "We have a baby brother!" I shout, hoping too late that no one is napping. The house is full, with Kyle's parents and Phillip and Miriam. Gretchen steps out of the kitchen and she hurries to me, taking the magazine. She reads over the information and looks at me. "I played with him for three years. He and his family lived above us in the same apartments where the Schweigers lived. When Ramona figured out who he was, we moved away."

"What are you going to do?" Gretchen asks.

"You mean what are *we* going to do," I say. I pull out my cell phone, and her eyes are big, watching me. For the rest of my life I'll wonder how all of this happened. I'll go through the what-if's countless times and settle on the same conclusion: I am seen. I dial the phone and put it on speaker so everyone can hear. Gretchen and I take our places in the wings, waiting. When a man's voice answers, Gretchen grabs my arm and we both smile.

The next act is about to begin.

DON'T MISS DONNA VANLIERE'S NEW NOVEL, *THE GOOD DREAM*

Coming in Spring 2012

Set in 1950s Tennessee, *The Good Dream* tells of one woman's unlikely path to motherhood, and of the power of secrets, vengeance and, ultimately, forgiveness.

Early Praise for *The Good Dream*

"*The Good Dream* is a great story of people saving each other in the unlikeliest ways. A heartwarming winner of a book."
—Jenna Blum, author of *Those Who Save Us*

"*The Good Dream* snares the reader right from the start. Donna VanLiere's pitch-perfect voice captures all the country charm and mystery of a long-ago time and place with its many acts of kindness and courage, as well as its secrets."
—Mary McGarry Morris, author of *Songs in Ordinary Time*

"Donna VanLiere shows she's not just for Christmas anymore."
—Richard Paul Evans, author of *The Christmas Box* and *Lost December*